BLANCO SOL

Other books by A. H. Holt:

Kendrick
Silver Creek

BLANCO SOL

•

A. H. Holt

AVALON BOOKS

NEW YORK

PRINTED IN THE UNITED STATES OF AMERICA
ON ACID-FREE PAPER
BY HADDON CRAFTSMEN, BLOOMSBURG, PENNSYLVANIA

For my mother,
Edna Mumford Haw

Chapter One

King bypassed a little town and worked his way southwest toward New Orleans. He made less than twenty miles most days and literally fell out of the saddle when he found a campsite. He managed to pull his saddle from Ranger's back, hobble him in the lush grass, and crawl in his blankets, too tired to think about fixing a meal. He waited until breakfast to make coffee most days.

This morning, dawn woke him. At first King couldn't remember where he was. He saw Ranger standing by the creek. Looking up at the thick branches of the live oaks, he rubbed his head several times and finally remembered. *I'm on my way home—it's still almost a thousand miles to Texas. I'll be there in a few weeks. Maybe I'll be well again by the time I get to New Orleans. Once I get well I'll make better time.*

Suddenly ravenous, he untied the cloth bag of food from behind his saddle. He had saved some bread and fried ham from his midday meal the day before. He finished the ham and one piece of the bread, saving enough to eat at noon so he wouldn't have to stop. When he finished eating he knelt awkwardly at the edge of the creek and drank from his cupped hands.

Ranger seemed glad to see him. "Come on, boy. We've got a lot of travel ahead of us. You won't be so fat and sassy when we get home. Those months you spent in the stable in Washington City almost ruined you."

King rode as though he belonged on horseback. He kept Ranger headed southwest and held him to a fast walk or a trot. The horse's long stride ate up the miles. Day after day he seemed to grow stronger. Unlike his rider, he showed no signs of weariness when they stopped at night.

Several days later, King rode into a little town where a shabby storefront announced: "TOWN OF BILDAD, LOUISIANA. Food, Drink, and Supplies." The three other buildings that made up the town seemed to be deserted. He couldn't see any people, but the door of the store stood wide open.

Tying Ranger to the hitch rack in front of the store, King limped across the porch and went inside. There were stacks of goods everywhere—mountains of bagged flour, beans, brown sugar, and salt. Guns, harness, and wagon parts decorated the walls. Anything you could think to ask for was there in abundance.

He approached the counter and asked the storekeeper, "How far is New Orleans from here?" The man was a thin, pasty-looking fellow with tobacco stains on his wispy beard.

"I'd say the city is about three days' travel, Mister, if you move right along. That is, if you're traveling horseback."

"I am, and I'm obliged to you. I need some decent clothes and a few supplies."

"Headed to Texas, I reckon."

"As a matter of fact, I am. Do the packet boats still make a regular run to Galveston?"

"They run twice a week now. Lots of folks going west. Ain't much to hold them around here no more. Them free blacks, backed by the army, is about taking over this far south. Most folks around these parts don't hold with that at all. Everybody that can scrape up travel money is going down this road, headed for Texas."

"You don't say. Well, I'll just collect up the things I need and get a move on."

King chose coffee, flour, salt, and bacon. He bought some heavy cord pants and riding gloves. A light carbine and sheath for his saddle and several boxes of shells completed his purchases.

The storekeeper eyed King's choices as he piled them on the counter. "You've been west before, ain't you, friend? Most folks ask me what they need. Then they buy all they can of what I say."

Watching the man's shifty eyes, King thought, *I'd bet they buy a lot of junk they'll never need.* Ignoring the storekeeper's comments, he added a wide-brimmed hat and a heavy wool blanket to his pile of goods and asked for his bill. He almost yelled out loud when he saw the total.

Ranger snorted and shied at the huge pack King tied to the back of his saddle. "Behave, you wild Cayuse. I'll get us a packhorse in Galveston. You'll be about enough trouble on a packet boat all by yourself. A little extra work won't hurt you one bit. Maybe it'll make you behave some better on the boat ride."

New Orleans seemed to be full of soldiers in Union blue. The sidewalks teemed with people, and the streets were crowded with every kind of cart and wagon and carriage that could be imagined. It seemed the whole town was trying to get somewhere in a hurry. King took Ranger to the first livery stable he found.

Shouldering his pack, he asked the old man who had taken his horse, "Can you direct me to a clean hotel, Uncle?"

Removing his pipe, the man asked, "You wanting to sleep or is you looking for some devilment?"

King laughed aloud and answered, "I want to wash off this trail dust and sleep until the next packet leaves for Galveston."

"Well, you better not be going to no hotel then. They's so much trash in this here town you got to sleep six to a room. Shore as shooting some sorry son will steal your gear while you's sleeping. You go round to number 8 Rue Saint Mary. Missus Glade takes roomers. She feeds good too. You'll be better off there, mister."

"I'm much obliged to you," King said, handing the man a

coin. He left the stable and slipped into the stream of people moving along the sidewalk. He soon found the house, and dropped his heavy pack on the porch to lift the big brass doorknocker. *This sure doesn't look like a rooming house*, he thought. It looked more like some planter's townhouse. King examined the imposing doorway with its frame of colored glass as he waited for someone to answer his knock.

The walls of the house were brick and stood three stories high. Wide windows reached from ceiling to floor on the porch level and were covered with fancy wrought iron. The little front yard had been clipped smooth and the flowers looked well-tended.

Beginning to feel nervous, King thought, *I wonder what that fella meant by sending me to this house?*

The door suddenly opened inward to reveal a handsome woman in the opening. She looked to be about thirty and wore a severe but attractive black dress. "Yes?" she asked in an icy voice. King noted that she obviously disapproved of rough-looking men with clumsy packs showing up at her fine door.

"I beg your pardon, ma'am." King removed his hat and bowed. "I'm Kingsley Sutherland from over in South Texas. An old black fella that works at Higgins' livery stable directed me to your house. I do apologize for bothering you. I see there must be some mistake. I was looking for a place to stay until the packet boat to Galveston leaves."

To King's astonishment, the woman smiled and opened the door a little wider. "Oh, Melton sent you to me. Do come in, Mr. Sutherland."

She turned to walk back into the hallway. King picked up his pack and followed as she led the way into a large room that was beautifully furnished as a parlor. King felt strange standing on the carpet. The room looked a lot like the ones he remembered seeing in houses in Charleston when he was a boy.

The woman crossed to seat herself behind a desk and said, "Please be seated, Mr. Sutherland. I'm Victoria Glade." She smiled invitingly and patted her glossy black hair into place. "I keep records here exactly like a hotel would. The town authorities require it. I must have your full name and your home address."

"You already have my name and I guess the nearest place I can call an address is San Antonio, Texas."

"You're actually from Texas. Well, my land, that's the first time I ever heard anyone say they were from Texas. Most people are on their way there."

"I really am from Texas, Mrs. Glade. I've, uh, I've been back east on business."

That'll just have to do. I'll never explain what really took me east to this fine southern lady.

"How long do you plan to stay with us, Mr. Sutherland?"

"Only till the next packet boat leaves for Galveston, please ma'am."

"That will be Friday. You'll owe me fifteen dollars for room and board for three days."

Wincing at the staggering sum, King paid the amount she asked. "Money sure don't go very far these days, does it?"

"Shouldn't be any surprise to you." Victoria Glade stood up. "It's been like this since the war ended. I'll get you some supper. Your room is the first one to the left at the head of the stairs. The door is open. There will be hot water in the wash-house out back so you can bathe after you eat."

King watched as she swung her skirts around and walked through the door. She was good-looking and she knew it. *It must be hard for someone like her to run a boarding house. No wonder she only took people sent to her by someone like Melton,* he thought.

A tiny black woman dressed in a white Mother Hubbard apron appeared in the door. "If you'll come to the kitchen, sir, Miz Glade says I'm to feed you." Her lined face was full of disapproval and her voice was as stiff as her starched apron.

Entering the kitchen, King seated himself at the long table. It was set with real china and silver as fine as the kind his mother owned. The woman served him a plate piled high with fried potatoes and ham. There was a plate of cornbread cut in huge squares on the table. A new mold of butter and a jar of pickles were within reach. The woman slammed a pitcher full of cold sweet milk down in front of his plate. By the time he'd eaten his fill the black woman had stopped working and was standing in front of the stove staring at him.

"I sure do thank you, ma'am. That was good. I've been eating rough and I was some kind of hungry. You're a great cook."

She seemed to lose some of her hostility at his smile. "You can eat, I'll say that for you. I guess it takes a lot to fill up a big man like you."

"Not usually as much as that. It really tasted good."

"I'm Ida. I'm Melton's wife. Miz Glade said he sent you over here."

"Yes, ma'am, he did. I left my horse at the livery stable and he said it would be better for me to come here than take my chances in a hotel."

King pushed his chair back and stood up. "I'll go up to my room now, Ida. Will you yell when my water is hot?"

"I'll knock on your door. It's bad enough Miz Glade done turned her home into a hotel. I don't have to go round yelling at people." She sniffed and tossed her head.

King chuckled as he left the kitchen.

His room held furnishings similar to the precious family pieces his mother had hauled across Texas. The huge bed was covered in hand-worked quilts. When Ida knocked on his door, King followed her downstairs and through the kitchen to a cabin in the yard. He soaked off the trail dust in a huge tin tub full of steaming water. He found a razor and strop hanging beside the mirror and shaved.

Staring in the mirror, he saw that his face had filled out again, but he looked older. Time had faded the livid scar and the sun had fired his skin until he looked almost as dark as an Indian. He thought he resembled his father. The scar didn't look too bad.

Dressed in his new tight-fitting trousers, King looked at

his shapeless and broken boots and almost laughed out loud. *I look like a spavined mule. I'd get laughed out of Texas in these boots. I'll have to get me a decent pair right away. There might be some smart-mouthed drover or two hanging around the docks in Galveston and I'd have to throw my gun.* Leaving the house, he walked slowly downhill, sometimes moving out into the street to get past groups of people crowding the sidewalks. After a few blocks he could see the empty masts of ships ahead. The wharf teemed with people, just like the streets.

King pushed his way past men in overalls standing beside women dressed in poke bonnets and calico. He also noticed flashily dressed men with smooth white hands and careful eyes. Cajun fish hawkers yelled from their boats. Children screamed and ran and climbed over the piles of boxes and baggage waiting to be loaded on the packet. He stepped over the barrier at the end of the gangplank and placed one tight new boot on the deck.

"Hold on there, dude," a voice yelled from the nearest door. "You can't just come on this boat without a by-your-leave."

A man rushed out onto the deck. He was dressed in tattered and filthy riding clothes, his face as red as fire from the heat of the cabin. His shaggy black hair made him look wild. He stopped in his tracks when he got close enough to see King's face.

"King Sutherland!" he whooped. "My God, man, you're supposed to be dead."

"Luke, I'm as alive as you are." King yelled with delight and held out his right hand.

Luke clasped King's hand in his and almost danced with excitement.

"Boy, it almost broke my heart when I talked to y'all's Mexican drover Eduardo in Santone. He told me your family had given you up for dead. Does your family know you're all right? Have you written to them?"

"Hey, hold on now, Luke—one question at a time. Let's go some place where we can talk."

"Aw, King. I can't leave this dang boat. I'm working my

passage back to Galveston. I come over on the cattle boat. Me and some old boys threw a little party last night and the blasted army threw me in jail. I ain't got enough money left to get home unless I work my way."

Luke hung his head and looked down at his scuffed and torn boots.

Slapping his friend's shoulder, King said, "I've got enough to see us home, Luke. I just paid for a cabin and space for my horse on this boat. We'll go see the captain and make arrangements for you."

"I reckon he'll jump at the chance to make a passenger out of me. I've lived on a horse so long I can't hardly walk on this boat with its everlasting rocking."

King told the captain that Luke wasn't going to work for him, bought passage for Luke, and led his friend to Rue Saint Mary. "I'll lend you some clothes so you can clean up decent. You can turn the legs of the pants up some. I've got enough to lend you some money for some new boots, too. Yours look like they might have been your granddaddy's."

"I been riding the grub line lately, old son. There ain't no money left in Texas to pay drovers. The cattle market went bust as soon as the war started and I've just been drifting lately. You know work is scarce for yore old pard Luke Wilson to sign on to wrangle cattle on a stinking boat."

"You can ride along home with me if you want," King offered. "Blanco Sol always needs riders."

"I'll shore trail along with you," Luke answered slowly. "Pards are as scarce as jobs these days."

King led Luke around the house to the wash-house and the bathtub. "You better clean up some before anybody sees or smells you, Luke. I shocked them bad enough when I showed up. You look like a wild Indian wrapped in rags. There's a cook here by the name of Ida that can make corn-bread so good you'll think you've died and gone to heaven. We don't want her upset none."

"Cornbread. That sounds good to me. I ain't been good and full since I can't remember when." Luke moaned in anticipation of the delights to come.

"You go ahead and get cleaned up and shaved. I'll go get you some clothes," King said.

He ran through the kitchen and up the stairs. As he came back down with his arms full of clothes he met Victoria Glade.

"Oh, ma'am, I ran into an old friend from my home. He's going to travel back to Texas with me. He hadn't found him a place to stay yet so I brought him back here with me. Can he share my room?"

"Of course he can, Mr. Sutherland. We're delighted to have your friend stay with us. There'll be a small extra charge, of course, for his meals." She was still dressed in black but had changed to a dress that bared her pale neck and shoulders. King tore his eyes away from the deep neckline.

She moved closer to him. "I'll be joining you for dinner this evening. Perhaps you'll have a glass of Madeira with me after we eat?"

"Why, sure thing, Miz Glade, I'd enjoy that." He wondered if the dress was for his benefit. *She sure is something*, he thought. *Supper might get to be real interesting*.

Luke was transformed when he strapped his old gun belt over the new clothes.

"Come on, man." King said. "If you'll try to hurry a little bit we can get you some respectable boots before dark."

The two Texans left the tanner's shop and sauntered along shoulder to shoulder. They were both lithe and handsome, and their skin had taken on a rich reddish-tan color from their days in the sun. Their clothes and new boots marked them as cattlemen—aliens in the hustle-bustle of the city.

"I'd shore hate to be stuck in this burg for long," Luke said as he looked into each passing face. "You can't hardly tell what kind of varmints you might meet."

"Don't you go getting touchy with anybody now, Luke. That boat leaves early Friday morning and we're going to be on her. There's too much law here for a drover to act natural."

"You can say that again. That doggone lieutenant that throwed me in jail would be dead if he'd been in Santone."

King laughed. "Still the same old fire-eater. You always stayed in trouble. I don't know how you managed to keep yourself alive this long without me to look after you."

"Aw, you laugh. Most of my gunplay started with you or Clint sparking some gal some other fella thought he owned."

"Look, Luke," King said, ignoring the jibe. "Here's a barbershop. It's still open. We could both do with a haircut."

They emerged from the shop some time later with their sideburns trimmed and their hair smooth. Except for the identical Navy Colts hanging low on their sides, they looked almost civilized.

"Let's get on back to that boarding house," King said. "I don't want to run into anybody else that knows me today."

"What in the world have you done to be on the dodge?"

"I'm not on the dodge. I'm a little bit afraid some Army man might recognize me. I should report to the garrison— it's kind of expected—but I don't want to be stranded here for weeks tied up in Army red tape."

"Why would the army care where you are?"

"They don't really. I've got papers showing my separation due to my injury, but I don't want to be bothered explaining myself."

"Well, come on then, we can hole up at your rooming house tonight and all day tomorrow. I don't want nothing more to do with them sorry blue boys myself."

Ida was almost finished putting supper on the table when the two men entered the dining room. "Sit down, y'all. Miz Glade will be down directly."

Luke moaned at the sight of plates piled high with fried chicken and delicately browned biscuits. The long table was almost covered with dishes: several bowls of vegetables, a gravy boat, a mold of butter in the middle of the table, a crystal dish of pickles, and another of applesauce.

"I can't believe what I see. Is it real?"

"It sure is, Luke. And I can swear that it tastes as good as it looks. Ida is the best cook in New Orleans, so her husband tells me."

"That fool. How would he know that?" Ida smiled her pleasure at King's compliments.

At that moment Victoria Glade walked in the door. Luke's eyes popped at the sight of her pearly white shoulders showing above the low neckline of her black dress.

"That's your landlady?" he sputtered. "I can't believe the luck some fellas have."

King pushed his chair back and he stood up, grabbing Luke and pulling him to his feet as well. "This is my friend I told you about, Miz Glade: Luke Wilson, from San Antonio. He's the best gun-toting cattleman in south Texas and he's saved my life more than once."

Luke turned red and mumbled, "How do, ma'am."

"I'm honored to meet you, Mr. Wilson. What an introduction! You must be pleased that you found Mr. Sutherland. Please take your seats, gentlemen."

Luke fell back into his chair and fastened his eyes on his plate. He didn't look up again until the meal was over.

As soon as everyone was served, Victoria asked, "Does your business take you east often, Mr. Sutherland?"

"Oh no," King answered, hoping Luke would maintain his silence. "I'm usually much too busy at home to travel. This was sort of an emergency trip."

"I want you to tell me all about Texas after dinner. People tell such outlandish tales. I'm sure I can trust you to tell me the real truth. Will you excuse Mr. Sutherland and me, Mr. Wilson?"

"Shore I will, ma'am," Luke replied, turning an accusing look on King. "I need my rest anyway."

Pushing his chair back, Luke stood up and bowed, his face serious and his cheeks still red. "I can't begin to say how great that meal was, ma'am. I'll be looking forward to breakfast."

"My room is the first on the left at the top of the stairs," King called as Luke hurried out of the room.

Victoria led King through a door off the central hall. "The other salon is only for entertaining my nosy neighbors and my husband's family," she explained. King wondered where this husband of hers was.

The room held French furniture upholstered in pale blue silk. The patterned carpet was so thick that King's boots sank in with every step. Victoria lit a lamp beside the sofa. "Come sit here beside me, Mr. Sutherland. We can enjoy the fire as we talk."

The room seemed almost too comfortable. King sat down and stretched his legs out toward the small fire in the marble fireplace. Victoria sat on the sofa near him. She turned his way, looking directly into his face and smiling as she listened to his tales of Blanco Sol Ranch and the part of Texas he'd grown up in.

King realized that her eyes were sad and hungry-looking. Tiny lines marred the beauty of her full mouth. Discontent and bitterness were written on her face. She dropped her hand to the seat of the sofa, her fingers almost touching King's knee.

"Won't you call me Victoria, Mr. Sutherland? I've been dying to call you King. It sounds so grand."

"That's real kind of you, Miz Glade, but I wouldn't feel exactly right acting so familiar all of a sudden. It surely ain't polite."

King stood up and held out his hand. "I reckon I'll just get on upstairs. I'll have to get up early to tend to some business and I'm downright tired from traveling. I've been looking forward to sleeping in that big bed, so I'll say goodnight."

Victoria Glade's eyes turned dark with anger, but she smiled and wished him a pleasant night.

King entered his room on tiptoe. Luke was already snoring. King slipped off his clothes as quietly as possible and slid under the quilts. He gently pushed Luke's inert body over to make room. He knew it wouldn't do to wake him— he'd surely raise a fuss.

King had no more than straightened out on the bed when sleep claimed him. He woke to rude shaking. Luke was already dressed. "Get up out of there, you lazy hog. Breakfast is long over. Are you going to sleep forever?"

"Get the heck out of here, you sorry no-good talking

machine. Can't you see I'm trying to sleep?" King turned his face to the wall and pulled the cover over his head.

"Ain't no need for you to cuss your friends just because you've been out tomcatting around all night," Luke taunted him.

"Oh, shut up. I have not been out tomcatting around and I ain't no kid for you to be trying to mind."

"Well, you shore act like one. Get dressed, will you? Let's get on that boat and stay there until it leaves. That high-stepping widow downstairs was making sheep's eyes at me at the breakfast table. Almost put me off my feed. I can smell trouble if we stay here a minute longer than it takes to get ourselves together and run."

"Aw, come on, Luke. You're lying. She wasn't flirting with you too?" King sat up in bed and looked into his friend's grim face. "No, I guess you're not lying at that. All right, get my pack while I dress. We'll put my horse on board and spend tonight on the packet."

The two men made short work of packing and slipped quietly down the stairs and out into the street. "Whew," said Luke. "Life is something, ain't it? A fella never can be shore what will happen when a good-looking woman's around."

King and Luke found a restaurant with an empty table and ate a huge meal. "Let's rustle on down to the docks," Luke said as he washed down his last bite of leathery steak with his second beer.

"We'll need some daylight to get your horse aboard the packet. If he's any good at all, he ain't going to want to take no boat ride."

"He might raise a fuss at that. He's a great horse. I wouldn't want him to hurt himself. I might have to bed down in the hold with him to keep him quiet."

"Don't you worry none about that. We'll hobble him and tie his head to the stall. He'll stand. Most horses are smart enough to not get hurt if they see they can't get loose."

The two men had to detour twice around groups of soldiers on the way to the livery stable. Luke's expression told King he might say something insulting to the men and get them in trouble. It didn't feel right to King for him to talk to Luke about his service in the Union army, but he would be forced to talk about it if the soldiers asked for their papers.

Melton wasn't at the livery stable, to King's great relief. He didn't want to have to explain to him why he was leaving early. A young boy led Ranger out into the yard for King to saddle him and tie his pack on.

Luke stood back and admired the horse. "That's a grand trail horse, King. He looks like he's strong and fast."

Luke was known as a good judge of horses. King had never known him to be wrong in his choice of a mount. He could pick out the finest horses in a remuda at a glance. Then he could get all the work a horse was capable of doing with his superb riding.

"Thanks, old man. That's fine praise coming from you. Ranger likes to show off, but he's strong and he's got a smooth gait."

The horse acted as though he was glad to see King and stood quietly for him to strap on his saddle and pack. "I'm going to buy a pack horse in Galveston, Luke. Say, where's your big red colt?"

"He's in Jake Benton's corral in Galveston. He's eating his head off, I reckon. He'll be too fat to run by the time I get back there."

"He'll lose the fat fast enough. I'm in a hurry to get back home."

King jumped into the saddle. "Here, Luke, climb up behind me. He can carry both of us easily."

King had to hold Ranger tight even with such a load on his back; he was skittish in the crowds of people. The loaded wagons and crowds of people seemed as numerous as they had been the first day he arrived in town.

When they finally reached the boat, Luke and King dismounted. Holding tight to Ranger's head, they led him onto the deck of the boat. A boatman rushed over to hand King two heavy pieces of canvas attached to a cable and quickly moved back several steps. "Lead him up beside that hole and get the straps under his belly," he shouted.

Luke looked at the man disdainfully. "Are you afraid of horses, fella?"

"You bet your boots I am, fella. I ain't fool enough to let one of them crazy nags kick my brains out."

Luke slipped Ranger's saddle from his back, placing it and his pack well out of the way of the horse's hooves.

"You hold his head, King. Look how he's rolling his eyes."

King held Ranger by his bridle and rubbed his quivering nose. He began to talk to him softly. "Take it easy, boy. We're not going to hurt you."

Luke slipped the canvas strips under the horse and attached them to the cable.

"Get out of the way," yelled the boatman. Two black men turned the pulley wheel, lifting Ranger clear of the deck. The great horse screamed in rage and fear. He kicked out with both hind feet, making the sling sway from side to side.

"Hold him still," Luke said quietly. "He'll calm down soon as he sees he caught."

King watched with his heart in his throat. One lunge at the wrong moment and he could lose Ranger.

Luke got the horse quiet finally, by just talking to him. "Let him down easy now," he cautioned the men on the pulley. He slipped into the hold beside the horse as they slowly let him down. "Come on now, boy. I'll put you in the best stall these folks have got since we're here first and then I'll give you a bait of grain."

Ranger stood stock still on the bottom of the boat with his head up, trembling all over. Luke's voice and hands soon calmed him and the danger was over. King felt as though he could hardly breathe until Luke climbed back up on deck.

"Stop your worrying, pard. Your precious horse is tied up like a baby. He'll be fine if this tub don't sink."

Chapter Two

The packet sailed in a gray mist before sunrise the next morning. Luke became helplessly ill with seasickness as soon as the boat started moving. King strode out onto the deck to watch the boat work its way through the crowded harbor. The mist cleared gradually as the sun burned through. King leaned his elbows on the rail and watched as the pilot eased his way along the marshy shoreline.

A clanging bell called King in to breakfast. The *Columbia* had once been used for passenger traffic only, but it had seen better days. The public rooms had been since partitioned off to make more cabins. The first settlers taking this crossing had been wealthy and fewer than the hordes of people traveling since the end of the war. Those early travelers had demanded white tablecloths and fine china. They enjoyed the services of uniformed waiters and stewards, and they ate like royalty and partied their way across without a thought of discomfort.

Today, the people huddled against the stern and crowding the dining room of the packet were mostly farmers and poor laborers. They were alike in that they wore tawdry clothes and carried poor-looking gear. Many didn't come into the dining room to eat. They had packed cold food to save money on meals.

King found a chair at the end of a table and sat down. His

interest was focused on the other passengers in the dining salon. The five men seated around the table were obviously brothers, close together in age. King had noticed them when they boarded in New Orleans. The youngest appeared to be in his late teens.

The boy reached to fill his plate with beef and potatoes from the platter a waiter placed in the center of the table. "Mind your manners, Ben," said the man at the head of the table. By his looks, King assumed he was the boy's older brother.

"Shucks, Neale, you're getting to be as bad as Ma used to be. I can't do nothing to suit you," complained the boy.

"You can try to remember what your ma taught you," said the man called Neale. "You'll be wild before we even get to Texas, at the rate you're going."

"Ease up on Ben, Neale," said the man to King's left. "He's getting too big for you to be dressing down in public."

The man then turned to King. "Pardon me, stranger. I'm Henry Hastings and these are my brothers. Are you going to settle in Texas too?"

King liked the looks of these men. He held out his hand. "I'm pleased you introduced yourself, Mr. Hastings. I'm Kingsley Sutherland. I'm on my way home to Texas. I've been east on business. My people have a ranch in a valley between the Frio and the Nueces, down south of San Antonio."

The Hastings, men and boy, began to all ask questions at once.

"How is the farmland around there?"

"Are there really herds of wild horses running free?"

"Have you ever killed an Indian?"

"Were you born in Texas?"

"Hey, wait. You boys just hold on a minute." Neale Hastings said, holding up his hands. "Mr. Sutherland will tell us about Texas. Let him talk."

"I'll tell you about myself first, then I'll try to answer your questions about the west. I'm from the Nueces country south of San Antonio. My father is a younger son of the Charleston,

South Carolina, Sutherlands. He couldn't be satisfied only being a part owner of a plantation or a shipping company, so he packed up mother and my brother, Clint, and me back in 1849 and took us west.

"We had plenty of money then so there was little hardship. We took one family of slaves with us. We also took some fine horses and a caravan of new wagons piled high with furniture and things to make us a home when we found a place. Clint and I made play of every mile.

"I guess it must have been awfully hard on my mother. She was a Ruffin, from Richmond, Virginia. She was raised a great lady, waited on hand and foot. I remember she was game, but the wagon travel and rough living had almost done for her by the time we got to San Antonio."

The youngest Hastings brother, the one called Ben, moved his chair closer to King and leaned on the table to watch his face as he talked.

"Dad put us up with a family of cousins there in San Antonio while he looked for a ranch to buy. He'd heard of land available south of San Antonio where Spanish holdings had been taken over by American settlers. He spent weeks riding off for days at a time, searching the countryside. A fellow named Red Henderson, a scout and guide who knew the country, rode with him.

"Dad finally found what he wanted: land that would support cattle and horses with plenty of water year-round. There was a house on the land and he painted a wild picture of the beautiful Spanish fort we could make into a wonderful home. He raved about the green savannas along the big creek near the place. He said they were dotted with the wild cattle that had been abandoned years ago by the Spanish.

"Mother was rested by then and eager to reach her new home. She left the comfortable home of our cousins in San Antonio, expecting to find a decent place to live waiting for her. The wagon trip took only a few days, nothing compared to the weeks of travel she had endured, but the weather turned cold and bitter. Rain slowed us down and made every creek and river crossing a nightmare with the wagons. When

we finally arrived, the huge barracks Dad had called a house
was stark and filthy. The rooms were like big stalls. Some of
them had actually been used to stable horses. The slaves had
to rout out everything from rats to skunks before we could
move out of the wagons.

"The house had been a fort for the Mexican army at one
time. It was built of some kind of light-colored stone and
adobe, laid out on a big square. The wooden gates in the
front open into a courtyard that measures about two hundred
feet each way. In the center of the courtyard is a pile of
stone under a big old cottonwood tree. There's a wonderful
spring that bubbles up into a clear pool in the roots of the
tree.

"Clint and I were in heaven, of course. We became about
as wild as Comanche Indians ourselves on the trip. It was an
adventure for us. I remember Mother standing there in the
rain, looking at the house, without saying a word. It was hard
work for her to make the ranch into a home, but she did it.
It's beautiful now. Quiet and cool and lovely, with Mexican
blankets hanging on the walls and soft Indian rugs on the
floors. There was some massive Spanish furniture in a few
of the rooms. We found long tables and huge, carved chests.
Mother arranged them in with the graceful stuff she brought
from Charleston and added the rugs and things and now the
house looks like a showplace. Its name is Blanco Sol, or, in
American, it's White Sun; you'll hear the riders and our
neighbors call it by either name.

"Clint and I learned to be *vaqueros*. There was a little
Mexican village at another spring not far from the house.
They raised our fruit and vegetables and helped Mother in
the house. We spent every moment that Mother didn't make
us study with a *vaquero* named Eduardo, learning to ride and
shoot and work cattle like he did.

"Dad had good fortune with his cattle and horses. He
brought some white mares and a stallion from over near
Durango, and hired Jim Wilson to care for them. Wilson's
son, Luke, was about my age and we became like brothers."

King and the men sat and continued talking long after the

table was cleared. The oldest Hastings brother, Neale, was the spokesman for the group.

"My brothers and I are from Tennessee. All of us, except for Ben here, served in the war. When we all finally got back home, alive and whole, we found our parents dead and our house and farm buildings burned. Ben was living with a neighbor and almost starving. We had no stock and no money to put in a crop, so we packed up Ben and headed south.

"We had two horses between us. Daniel and Henry sold them for enough money to buy supplies and decent shoes for us to walk in. We've been at it over two years, getting ourselves this far and paying to get on this boat. We kept traveling and working whenever we could find someone to hire us. We hope to find work when we land in Galveston and save up enough money to get us a start somewhere."

King felt drawn to these strong young men. They were broke, but proudly asking only a chance to work to make their place. "Do you men know anything about cattle?"

"Only what any boy growing up on a farm learns," Neale said. "We had horses and mules and oxen. Henry here can handle six mules teamed to a wagon like going away. Daniel always thought he was old Daniel Boone himself come back to life. That boy can handle a rifle better than anybody I've ever known. The rest of us are just plain farmers, but we're strong and willing to learn any honest work."

King's mind whirled as he weighed the idea of this group of stalwart young men at Blanco Sol Ranch. His father had hired American riders several times through the years but most of them were crooked or drunks. He always ended up firing them, if they didn't just drift off of their own accord after a payday.

The cattle market was bound to open up now that the war was over. With men like these working, they could brand and sell some of the thousands of wild Mexican cattle that ranged along the canebrakes of the creeks and rivers.

"I'd like to offer you men a deal. My father's ranch always needs hands. I'll buy a wagon in Galveston and hire a

Mexican to guide you to our ranch. If Dad will hire you to work our cattle, agree to stay with us for a year. If he won't hire you, I'll give you the wagon and supplies so you can move on somewhere else."

The brothers silently looked at one another.

"Well?" Neale asked, looking at his brothers.

"Yes." Henry and Daniel answered together.

"Oh, Neale. Please say yes," begged Ben, his eyes shining with excitement.

The last brother simply nodded. Neale stood up and held out his hand. "It looks like we're your men, Mr. Sutherland."

King shook Neale Hastings' hand with satisfaction.

"People call me King, Neale. You boys wait for me on the dock when we get to Galveston."

King returned to his cabin, smiling to himself. "Are you dead, Luke?" he yelled as he opened the door.

"Ohhh, please shut up." Luke groaned. "I wish I was dead. King—promise me if I ever try to get on a boat again you'll throw your gun on me." He raised himself up on one elbow. "Are we there yet?"

"Shucks, we just got started good. We'll be there soon enough. Get yourself out of that bunk. There's some people I want you to meet."

"I don't ever want to meet anybody again." Luke flopped over to face the wall. "Drag me off of this rocking torture chamber when we dock."

"You'd feel better if you got some air."

King left Luke feigning sleep and took up his post at the rail. His thoughts were a jumble. He knew it was possible that his father might throw him out when he reached the ranch. He wondered what the Hastings brothers would do when they found out he had fought for the Union. Luke never even mentioned it. It would surely all come out when they reached Blanco Sol.

No one crowded the Galveston docks. The island didn't look a lot different than it had the last time King had been there, more than five years earlier. The place had grown a little. The stores were fairly busy and he saw a new hotel as he, Luke, and the Hastings brothers started the mile and a half to the Benton place.

"Get up on Ranger, Luke. You'll never make it trying to walk."

Luke nodded and clambered into Ranger's saddle, his remarkable horsemanship holding him there despite his condition.

Benton was sitting on the porch of his trading post when the cavalcade walked into his yard. He heaved his huge body upright and stepped forward to peer at King.

"It's King Sutherland. Alive, by all that's holy!" His voice boomed.

"I sure feel alive now, Benton. It's great to be back home and it's good to see you."

"Where in the name of goodness have you been for so long, boy? Your people believe you were killed over two years ago." Benton reached for King's hand and wrung it in both of his.

"I've been laid up. I got this nasty whack on my head after the surrender and I've just now gotten myself well enough to get back."

Benton looked askance at King's explanation but he didn't ask questions.

"Come on inside, King. I'll stand you a drink. It ain't often a dead man walks in here."

King followed Benton into a huge, dark room piled high with trade goods.

"Who's that crowd of tall fellas with you? Not counting Luke Wilson, of course."

"They're the Hastings brothers from Tennessee. They're going to Blanco Sol with me to learn the cattle business."

"They look like they'll make fine cowhands if you can keep them. You'll need them too. Cattle are moving through here again. It's about time. For a few years there I thought I'd go broke for sure. Nobody in the country had two coins to rub together.

"I heard folks saying that a half-breed cowman name of

Jesse Chisum drove cattle north this past summer. Some guy named Joe McCoy is supposed to be buying cattle for the railroad up in Abilene. It's almost a thousand miles of rough country, dangerous river crossings, and Indians, but that McCoy paid eight dollars a head. There'll be cattle by the thousand going up that trail next spring."

"You mean this McCoy will buy all the cattle he can get? What does he do with them?"

"He's got good grass and plenty of water. He built corrals and holds those trail-ganted cattle long enough to fatten them back up some, then he puts them on a train to Chicago."

"The railroad comes to Abilene now?" King was stunned. It seemed he had been out of his head for five years. "Benton, I can't take it in. It seems to me the whole world has changed since I left Texas in '62."

Still shaking his head, he dickered with Benton for a heavy wagon and four mules for the Hastings brothers to use on the trip to the ranch. After buying supplies and a packhorse for himself and Luke and a larger order of supplies for the Hastings, he asked Benton if he could recommend an honest Mexican to guide the family cross-country to Blanco Sol.

"Juan Marcel is out back. You remember him, and you know he can be trusted. He's been all over all that country. I'll call him."

Marcel agreed to lead the Hastings brothers to Blanco Sol. King helped them load and wished them goodbye. After shaking hands with King and Luke, they trooped off to the wagon and climbed aboard, their eyes filled with excitement.

"Them boys are shore attached to one another, ain't they?" Luke stood on the porch watching the wagon leave.

"I'll be glad to see them when they reach the ranch, Luke. We've got a fortune to make and we're going to need their help."

"Have you gone loco? How can five Tennessee farm boys help us make a fortune?"

"We're going to round up some of those wild Mexican cattle out of the brakes of the creeks and the rivers and drive them north. Benton told me about Jesse Chisum's drive up to Abilene."

"Shucks, that ain't no news. I was riding with Chisum last spring when he got that fine idea."

"You rode with Chisum? Why'd you quit?"

Luke leaned one shoulder against the side of the log building and rolled a cigarette before he answered. "That Indian is a pure crook. He makes anybody he rides with turn into a cattle and hoss thief and I ain't hankering to end up swinging from the end of a rope."

"Those are hard words, Luke. Chisum would draw on you for less."

"Well, I reckon Jess Chisum would have enough hoss sense not to draw on me." Luke's hand fell to his gun. He settled it more comfortably against his leg.

"I guess you're right at that, but he might not worry about an even break if he is a horse thief."

"Chisum don't give breaks of any kind. I figure to just stay out of his way until he gets killed. It's coming. Lately he's working for some rancher called Cole over east of Santone. He's helping that fella drive off small ranchers, steal their stock, and put his brand over top of theirs. I couldn't stand for a play like that.

"I met a brother and sister in Santone. They'd been running a small spread in the canebrakes just south of Cole's range. He warned them off. When they wouldn't run he and Chisum rode out with some more old boys and drove that Jerdone family out of their cabin at gunpoint. They fired the place. Right in front of them. I couldn't tell them kids I rode with Chisum. It stuck in my craw. I just sloped back to the bunkhouse and collected my gear. I been riding grub line and scratching for enough money for smokes ever since."

"What's become of the ranchers that Cole fellow ran off?"

"Those Jerdone kids were right there in Santone when I left. The boy, Roy his name is, got work at the stage depot. The girl is tending her folks. They moved into one of them

Mexican shacks down on the flats. I figure to drop in on them when we pass through."

"I'd like to meet them. That's hard luck. Most ranchers treat the open range like it's theirs by right, but I never heard of people being run off by force before."

"Well, wake yourself up, pard. Texas has some changed since you left." Luke shook his head. "If you ain't been practicing with that Colt you're packing, you better get started. Guns are going to be all that stands between decent folks and ruin in the next few years, or I'll eat my hat for breakfast."

King was thoughtful as he and Luke started off for San Antonio. He had left some money with Slinger Doan at the saloon there. He knew it would be waiting for him if Slinger were still alive. It wasn't much, but the money he left Washington City with was beginning to run a little low.

As they got ready to turn their horses out of Benton's yard, a wagon train passed on the road to San Antonio, where it would meet up with a larger train headed for Santa Fe and California. King counted twenty-six wagons. They were all new and covered with bright canvas. Each wagon had a four-mule hitch pulling it. Here and there men were mounted and extra horses were tied behind some of the wagons. The faces of the men glowed with excitement. Their eyes seemed to strain ahead to see beyond the trail.

There were women on most of the wagons, their dark dresses and bonnets standing out against the light-colored canvas on the wagons. Their faces looked tired. The journey was only beginning and their eyes were already dull with weariness. King shook his head. He knew some of them wouldn't make it. The ones that did would find hardships enough with the land and weather and Indian trouble. Now it looked like they'd have to fight big ranchers like that Cole fellow.

They reached Big Spring at sundown, far ahead of the slow-moving wagon train. The trail ran through spotty groves of timber. Giant oaks shaded the area near the spring.

Luke made a fire and started stirring biscuits in a battered

tin pan he pulled out of a pack behind the saddle on his sorrel. King unsaddled the horses and hobbled them in the lush
grass nearby. As he walked back to the grove, Luke called
out, "The grub will be ready in a minute. Watch this bacon
for me while I dig a can of peaches out of my pack."

The simple meal over, they cleaned up and repacked their
pans and tin plates. They had enough biscuits and bacon left
over for a cold breakfast.

Luke threw more wood on the fire. "There, that ought to
last a while." He unrolled his blankets beside the fire and sat
down, stretching out his long legs. "Pull up a stump, King.
There's some things you need to know before we ride into
Santone."

King placed his unrolled bed near Luke's and sat down,
drawing his knees up under his chin. "Don't look so serious,
old man. These last years have been hard and I'm sure glad
to be back here looking at a campfire. I'm feeling almost
like King Sutherland again for the first time in years, but I
can sure feel trouble brewing when you look at me like that."

"You've got trouble, all right. Things have been going
from bad to worse with your family. White Sun Ranch shore
ain't what it was when you left."

King rolled a cigarette, took one long drag, and threw it in
the fire. "Just go ahead and tell me, Luke."

"Well, to start it off, your dad's been real bad sick. He had
him a stroke of apoplexy almost a year ago. I hear he still
can't walk no farther than a chair under the cottonwoods
there in the courtyard."

"Oh no." King dropped his head in his hands, then asked
in a husky voice, "Is Mother all right?"

"Aw, sure she's all right, King. She never went back on
you neither. I rode into White Sun in the spring of '64. Your
ma acted plumb glad to see me. She always did treat me like
another one of her boys. She read me your letters. Your dad
wouldn't even open his mouth to speak to me. When I
walked into the courtyard he got up and stomped off like he
couldn't stand the sight of me."

Tears clouded King's eyes at the picture of his mother

reading his letters to Luke. She had been hurt when he chose to fight for the enemies of her people, but she said she was a mother before she was a Southerner and his choice could make no difference in her love for her oldest son. She would welcome him back with joy. He was sure of that.

"Dad's still bitter about the way I left. That's hard to hear. And he's sick. That's the worst blow life could hand to a man like him. He was always more man than me or Clint. For him to be laid low by illness has to be terrible for him." King shook his head and looked at Luke. "Clint's running the ranch?"

Luke's face was grimmer than ever at the mention of Clint's name.

"What is it, Luke? Tell me."

"I hate this. You know Clint's always been a little soft. He hasn't had anybody like you to keep him straight like you did when we were boys. There's been no money from cattle these last few years, so he fell in with a bunch of hard riders and trapped and broke wild horses for the Confederate Army. He stayed away from the ranch for months at a time.

"There was some talk in Santone that he was involved with old Hank Billings in horse stealing and other things. Most folks were afraid to say anything about it while your dad was still out and about, but it kept cropping up.

"Clint came back to the White Sun Ranch to stay in late '64. I guess he figured the way the war was going. He got to running around with that Spaniard, Don Alvaraz over to Riza, and finally married his daughter."

"Clint's married to Mercedes Alvaraz? Well. She was always saying Clint would never amount to anything without me. When I left home she swore she'd wait for me."

"You can't expect no woman to wait when you're dead, you fool. Especially not that beautiful, black-eyed Spanish doll. She cut a wide swath through all the boys before she married Clint, I'll tell you that."

King was shaken by the picture Luke's words painted. He thought of Mercedes' soft white arms around his neck. She had met him at an old cabin on the ranch many times that last summer. They had spent hours together. He'd hardly thought of her for years. Now she was married to his brother.

"Well, it's a fact I sure haven't any room to feel jealous of Clint for his good fortune, but I have to admit that I do a little. I'll get over it before I get home, though. It would take more than Mercedes Alvaraz to come between us."

Luke looked into King's eyes. "Brace yourself, old son. Something else will sure come between you and Clint, unless you've changed an almighty lot."

"What now?" King felt a real fear clutch at his heart.

"Clint still rides out with that Billings bunch. He leaves in the night and comes back the same way. He leaves broke and comes back flush. Every time, a wagon train or stage is held up and robbed."

"Luke you're crazy!" King yelled. He jumped up to face Luke. His body was trembling with rage, and he held his left hand out from his body, hovering over the butt of his Colt. "You're a liar," he choked out.

"Shore you can't draw on me, pard." Luke held his arms straight out, hands palm-up. "I laid my gun over there on my pack before I braced you with this."

"Go get it, blast you." King trembled with fury. "That's a lowdown, sneaking coward's trick. I ought to shoot you down like a dog."

"I ain't going to fight you, King. I know it's hard to swallow hearing that your brother is such a skunk, but it's true."

"You can't be sure of that." King was calming down. As his sudden fury died, his brain began to work again. "There's got to be another explanation."

"No, King." Luke shook his head. "There ain't no other explanation. Clint and Billings have teamed up with that Spaniard Alvaraz. They're robbing stages and an occasional wagon train. They're killing every witness, too. People are on to them. It's only a matter of time before Clint's caught and hanged. I know it's hard, but you've got to face it."

King dropped his hand away from his Colt and staggered away from the light of the fire. Flopping down under a tree, he burned and shook with anger at Luke and fear for Clint. *My brother is a thief and a murderer—a murderer of innocent women and children?* He thought it over and over. The horror of it would surely drive him crazy. After a while, King got control of himself and returned to the campfire, his face white and cold. Luke had replenished the fire and was sitting in the same place.

"Luke, forgive me." He walked to Luke's side and held out his hand. Luke's face broke into a smile and he grabbed King's hand, standing up as he did so.

"Aw, there ain't nothing to forgive. I don't blame you for going wild at hearing such news. It would be more than I could stand still for."

King reached out and folded Luke's shoulders in his arms. "I can't believe anything would make me threaten to draw on you. We've been friends so long we're like brothers, and for a minute there I would have killed you."

"Forget it, boy." Luke laughed shakily. "I ain't so easy to kill. Even for you."

Neither man talked much as they prepared for sleep. King lay awake agonizing over what he could do about his brother. It was almost morning before sleep closed his eyes.

The rest of the trip to San Antonio was pleasant and uneventful. King didn't feel like talking and Luke didn't bother him. The country was different as they neared the town. There was plenty of grass, but trees were scarce except near the river. King and Luke skirted a wagon train camped just outside the town.

"Them settlers are getting thick," said Luke. "The Comanche and Kiowa are going to have themselves a rare old time."

"Do the Indians attack big trains like that?"

"Naw. They wait for something easier than that. Anything less than thirty wagons and an escort of troopers is committing suicide to leave here though."

The town bustled with life. Wagons rumbled up and down

the dusty street. The board sidewalks were busy with people. Horses were tied in front of several buildings.

"Look at that bunch of horses there in front of the saloon." Luke pointed to a hitching rail in front of a big two-story building.

"They look like Quivira stock to me."

"You shore ain't lost your eyesight. They're Quivira horses all right. I wonder what those boys are doing so far from home. Let's get down and go in here."

King and Luke tied their horses at the rail and walked into the saloon. The room was dim, and it took a moment for their eyes to get used to it.

As soon as he could see clearly, Luke yelled. "Hey, you old fire-eaters, look what I drug in from Galveston."

A group of men sitting around a large table stood up as one, astonishment written on their faces. After a second's hesitation, they rushed forward to shake King's hand, pound his back, and yell their greetings.

"Where the blazes have you been?"

"Come back from the dead."

"You old hoss thief, where've you been hiding?"

King felt warm with happiness at the greetings of these men. It helped heal the deep hurt and shame he felt over Clint.

"Let's sit down and have a drink together, boys."

King grabbed a chair and sat down at the table. "Get us a bottle, Luke, and tell Slinger to make it decent whiskey, not this rot-gut these boys have been drinking."

The faces of the group of cowhands were tanned as dark as Luke's and King's. The creases at the corners of their eyes and roughened skin showed the ravages of hard years in the saddle.

"Tell us what happened to you, King." The speaker was Windy Mason, so called not for talking, but for riding like the wind on fast horses. King looked at their open, friendly faces. He could see no hint of any feeling against him because of his loyalties during the war or the stories about his brother.

"I got hurt, boys. It was a head wound. You can see the scar here. I was plumb loco for months. I woke up one day with a clear head and as soon as I got strong enough I beat it for home as hard as I could ride."

"That's hard luck, King," said Charlie Bull, the half-breed.

Bill Ewell, the ageless senior member of the group, raised his glass.

"Here's to good friends. I'm plumb glad you made it through, King."

"Thanks, Bill. A man needs his friends. What are you boys doing in Santone?"

"We're just drifting. We been riding for Dave Williams over to Cottonwood until he fired Charlie and Matt here for fighting. We all quit. It won't much of a job no-how. Williams ain't sold five hundred head of cows in the last five years. The pay and the grub were so poor we shore won't miss either one."

"Have you boys heard tell about that fellow Joe McCoy that's buying cattle up in Abilene?"

"We heard, King," answered Bill. "Welton Smith stopped in here earlier today telling everybody that his pa sold four hundred head of scrub stock for eight dollars a head up there back in August. He took them up the trail behind that half-breed Jesse Chisum."

"How many head could we drive if we had, say, twenty drovers, Bill?"

"What are you thinking? That's a long, hard trail, King. You shore can't hit it with winter coming on."

King shook his head as he leaned forward. "Let me explain what I'm thinking."

The men leaned forward in their chairs and silently watched his face.

"The valley is full of wild cattle. They're almost a pest on Blanco Sol. If I could get together enough riders to clean some of them out of the brakes and brand about a thousand head, we could drive them north early next spring. I'm feeling that the trail Chisum laid out will be as busy as New Orleans come next May. My idea is to get ready this winter and get the jump on the other outfits."

"Well, King, that's sure a fine idea," Bill said. "No offense to you, but there's one fly in the ointment."

"What's wrong with it?"

"We shore can't ride for White Sun Ranch as long as Clint Sutherland is there."

King felt a wave of anger and then shame for his brother. "Is there no doubt in your minds about Clint, boys? Isn't it just possible that people are wrong in what they're saying about him?"

"There's always some doubt, King, until a man's caught red-handed, but we ain't never rode for no crooked rancher and Clint's got the name of one, whether it's true or not."

King clenched his hands on the table. His feelings were still too new for him to trust his reactions. Everyone at the table was quiet for a moment.

Luke spoke up, looking around the table. "King Sutherland will be running White Sun Ranch in a few days, boys. Give him a few weeks' start. He'll straighten out this thing about his brother or he'll stop the talk."

Bill Ewell spoke for the Quivira men. "We'll ride to the end of the earth for you, King. Me and the boys will hole up here with Luke and show up at White Sun in November."

King shook hands with each man. He and Luke went outside to their horses.

"Luke, you can't desert me now. I'll need you with me when I face Clint."

"You've got to ride this bronc alone, boy. I can't mix in between you and your family."

"I didn't want us to ever be parted again, Luke, but have it your own way. I'll be expecting you all in November."

Luke watched King mount and reached up to rub Ranger's neck. "Take good care of this horse, King. I'll be at White Sun in November if I ain't dead. I'm going to look up that Jerdone family I told you about."

"Didn't you say something about there being a sister? Don't tell me you've gotten over being afraid of girls?" King grinned down at Luke's red face.

"Everybody can't be a ladies' man like you. Get along now, you'll have to push to get to Spanish Wells by nightfall." Ranger covered the miles to Spanish Wells before nightfall. King felt tempted to push him on to get home earlier, but the small packhorse showed signs of being tired. The well lay beside the ruins of an old Spanish church. He led Ranger through the crumbling stones scattered on the ground to reach a small patch of grass where he could graze. King had to haul water for Ranger and the packhorse in a canvas bag he kept behind his saddle. Someone had stolen the bucket from the well.

King muttered aloud, "I'll have to bring another bucket the next time I come through here. I sure can't imagine what kind of coyote would steal a water bucket."

His camp felt lonely without Luke. King made his supper of jerky and water. He thought it best not to risk a fire. *Some Indian might spot it and I wouldn't have a chance against a hunting party sitting here by myself*, he thought.

One more day of hard riding and King was on Blanco Sol property. He made a dry camp near some willows along an old creek bed. Ranger snorted his discontent with the scant hatfull of water King gave him. The pace was telling on the packhorse. *It's a good thing I'll reach the ranch house early tomorrow.* King thought as he watched the animals drink their small ration of water.

King contented himself with a few sips of water from his canteen. He decided not to eat. The jerky would cause too much thirst. He leaned back against his saddle and was asleep in minutes.

Chapter Three

At dawn King broke camp. He rode only a few miles before he crested a hill and could see the ranch house. Bright sun reflected off its high walls, making it appear to be painted a dazzling white. He pulled Ranger to a stop and stared. His eyes blurred with tears. "What a sight—I can't believe I forgot how beautiful it is. Not even for one minute."

It took almost an hour to reach the house. King rode around to the back gate. It hung open and looked as though it hadn't been painted since he left. He dismounted and tied Ranger to the post. Using his hat, he knocked some of the trail dust from his clothes.

I guess they'll recognize me. I haven't changed all that much, he thought. He ran his fingers along the scar across his forehead. *Mother will sure cry over that, but there's no help for it now.*

King strode into the courtyard, his boot heels sounding on the flagstones and his spurs jingling with every step. The courtyard looked exactly the same. Taking off his hat, he walked toward the woman sitting on the bench beside the spring.

Her face was turned away. When she heard his step, she turned and stood up, peering at him through the shadows under the cottonwood. Katherine Sutherland was tall for a woman, and still beautiful.

King stopped a few feet from her and whispered, "It's me, Mother."

Her face working, Katherine held her hands over her heart. She took a step forward and cried out his name. King reached out and she fell into his arms. He led her gently back to the wide bench. She stared up at him, clutching his arm with both hands.

"Are you real?"

"I'm real, Mother, I'm real." King reached down to kiss her cheek and held her close in his arms. She wept aloud.

"Let me look at you, son." She lay one white hand on King's forehead, over the scar. "What happened to your face?"

"That's what held me up so long, Mother. It was a saber cut. I got it after the surrender. I was working crowd control in Washington City, and some men got a little crazy. My left leg was broken too, but I was out of my head for so long that it was completely healed when I woke up. All I had to do was rebuild my strength once I came back to the land of the living.

"That's almost seven months back now. I sent you and Dad a letter then and another when I got back in good enough shape to start out for home."

"I can hardly take it in that you're really here, son. It's been so long. I waited and waited for a letter, but we haven't received one. No one from the ranch has been to town for months. After the war ended, I looked for you for months. Clint finally convinced me I was only torturing myself. I finally began to believe that you had been killed in those last months of the war."

"Well, I'm at home now. I expect to stay here for a while, too. Mother, will Dad be willing to accept me back?"

Katherine shook her head. "Didn't you know he had a severe stroke?"

"Luke told me that. How bad is he?"

"Your father is a shell of the man he was. He can get around with a cane, but he hasn't regained his speech. He's just given up."

"I can't believe Dad would ever stop fighting."

"He has. I believe he could live his life normally again if he would only try. He had so much strength, but he's lost his will. He'll only hobble out here for a few hours each day. He spends the rest of the time in that big chair in his room. He refuses to even look at Clint and the only time he notices me is when he pounds on the floor with his cane and points at something he wants." Sobbing, Katherine dropped her head in her hands. King kept his arm around her and waited until she stopped crying.

"Come on now, Mother. Dry your eyes. I'm dirty and hungry. It's a long, dry road from San Antonio."

"Oh, King, of course, I'll get Elena to fix you some breakfast. Go to your old room, dear, everything is just as you left it." She wiped her face and smiled up at him. "I'm all right now."

King ducked his head under the porch and opened the door to his room. It was like stepping back into a world forgotten. His books and rifle were where he had left them. Either his mother or their housekeeper, Elena, had cleaned around his things without moving them. He closed the door and sat down on the bed. The feeling of going back in time was almost frightening.

The last time he spoke to his father was the day in '62 when he left to join the army. Lambert Sutherland had been furious. He had stormed at King, "You're nothing but a traitor. You'd shame me in front of the world by joining the Yankee Army? How could you do your mother this way? You'll be fighting your mother's people and mine. Would you kill your own family?"

King had tried to explain how he felt. He believed the Union had to be saved at all costs. Slavery was dying and the nation was more important than Southern pride.

"Southern pride!" his father roared, slamming his hands on the table. "If you had any pride at all, you'd crawl off somewhere and die of shame. If you do this thing you're no son of mine. You disgrace the name of Sutherland. I'll give this ranch to Clint."

Hurt and angry, King shouted his defiance to his father. "I'm doing what I think is right. That's what you've always taught me to do."

"Don't you ever say I taught you anything, you lowdown coyote. Get out of my house." King left his father tearing his hair and cursing him. He kissed his mother goodbye and rode off, wondering if any war could be important enough to make his father hate him.

A knock on the door yanked him back to the present. He opened the door to reveal the grinning face of their black rider, Jeff. He labored with a huge tub of hot water. "Look out, now. This here is hot enough to scald you."

He placed the tub near the fireplace and, turning, pulled off his sombrero. "It's shore fine to have you home, Mr. King. You been needed here."

"Jeff, I'm plain grateful to be home. Stick out your hand, man. I'm glad to see you."

Jeff took King's hand wordlessly.

"Don't call me Mister King anymore, Jeff. You're a free man now. Call me King like the rest of the riders do."

"I know all about that stuff, Mr. King. But you ain't never treated me no way but family no-how. Things won't never change for me. I'll always belong to White Sun."

"How are things on the range, Jeff?"

"It's been real bad the last few years, there's cattle everywhere, but the weather's been dry and the hosses have suffered some. What hosses we got left."

"What do you mean, what horses we've got left?"

"Hoss thieves, that's what I mean. The *vaqueros* and me have been riding four-hour turns watching what's left of them for over a year. There was a big raid early last summer. We lost over a hundred head in one night."

King was stunned. "Clint didn't try to get them back?"

"I reckon surely he did, but he didn't let me ride with him."

"Are you hinting at something, Jeff?"

Jeff looked frightened. "I ain't hinting exactly. I know. Something bad is going on and Clint knows something about it."

"I heard things in Santone. Do you think any of the talk about Clint and the Billings bunch and that Alvaraz is true?"

"Well, shore it's true about Hank Billings and that Alvaraz."

"I'm afraid it will prove to be true about Clint as well." King shook his head sadly. "It's hard to believe. Will you take care of my horses and gear for me, Jeff? I'll take a walk down to the bunkhouse later."

"I saw that big black tied up out yonder. He's a fine hoss." Jeff's eyes showed his love of horses. He reached his hand out and touched King's shoulder as he left the room.

King bathed and dressed in a pair of trousers from his closet and a blue shirt that had always been his favorite. As soon as he was ready, he left his room and walked along under the porch roof to the entrance to the dining room. That room also looked exactly the same as he remembered. He took the chair where a plate and silver were set.

He had no more than seated himself when he heard heels tapping and Mercedes ran in the door. She was dressed in riding clothes, a white shirt with a black leather vest and a divided skirt. Her black hair was pulled severely back from her face, and her dark eyes were huge against her white skin.

"King!" she shrieked. He jumped up to catch her as she threw herself into his arms.

"Oh, King, I thought you were dead. Oh, my darling, where have you been?" Her arms were tight around his neck. She kissed him over and over.

"Hey, take it easy, girl." King caught hold of her arms to push her away. "Where's Clint?" he asked, looking into her eyes.

"I don't care where he is now. You are here." Mercedes tossed her head and set her mouth defiantly.

"Well, you shore better start caring. He's your husband." King turned his back on her and took his seat at the table.

Mercedes flopped down in the chair beside King and reached out to catch one of his hands in hers. "Don't turn away from me, King. I love you. I've always loved you. I married Clint because I believed you were dead."

His face red with anger, King leaned toward her and almost snarled his words. "Keep quiet, Mercedes. You're my brother's wife. That's the end of it. Don't ever say such a thing to me again."

Mercedes jumped to her feet. Her face contorted with fury. Her Spanish blood and pride colored her words. "You filthy traitor. You will be sorry for this. I will break your precious mother's heart."

King reached out and caught her arm, pulling her back close to him. "I'm afraid to ask what you think you know, girl, but if you open your vicious mouth to my mother, I'll kill you." His words were spoken softly, but his tone was frightening. "I mean it, Mercedes. Don't think I'm still the lovesick boy you led a dance. I'll break your neck." He threw her arm away from him. "Get the devil out of here."

Mercedes ran sobbing from the room.

"What was all that about?" Clint stepped in the dining room door just after Mercedes ran out. "Mercedes was crying. What did you say to her?"

King was staggered at the difference in his brother. His face showed signs of hard living; there were dark circles under his eyes and his skin had a yellowish cast.

"She was only glad to see me back home and in one piece, Clint. You know how hysterical she can get. How about you?"

Clint stood in the doorway and stared at King. "You haven't changed much. That scar won't hurt you any with the girls, either." Clint hesitated a moment before he said, "Yes, brother. I'm glad to have you back home." He smiled and looked more like the younger brother King had always loved, in spite of his weakness for drink.

"Come sit down with me, Clint. I've been trying to eat. If anyone else comes in, I'll probably starve."

King watched Clint take a chair across the table from him. "Tell me what's going on around here. Jeff said we lost most of Dad's horses."

"Yes, we did lose some." Looking down at his hands, Clint continued. "Most of the Durango whites are gone— over a hundred in all. Hank and I tracked them to the border.

We were ambushed just north of the Rio Grande and had to shoot our way out. Luck was all that saved us. We had to ride like the wind to escape with our lives."

Feeling almost sick, King accepted Clint's statement without further questions. He thought Clint looked like he was lying. He had never been able to look King in the eye and tell a lie with a straight face. Watching the play of emotion on his brother's face, King finished his breakfast. He prayed he would be able to get Clint out of the mess he had made for himself—if it wasn't already too late.

Clint suddenly looked across the table at King and said, "Tell me about what happened to you, King. Where have you been so long?"

King told his story again, slipping back into his role as hero to this boy he had loved and watched over most of his life. He and Clint fell to recalling incidents of the past and laughing together over escapades they had shared. Watching Clint relax and become more like the boy he had known before the war was bittersweet for King. Clint's light brown hair still hung into his blue eyes. When the lines of dissipation around his mouth and eyes relaxed he looked ten years younger.

"This is great, Clint, but I've got to go face Dad," King said eventually.

"Don't do it, King. He's a walking dead man. If you stay out of his way he'll never know you're in the house. The sight of you might kill him."

"That's an awful thing to say to me, boy. I've got to see him. I can't slink around like a coward. He wouldn't expect me to."

"He won't expect anything. He's like a stick of wood. I always lived in terror of him before he had that stroke. He seems pitiful to me now."

"Maybe seeing me will shock him to life again. Anyway, I've got to face him, whatever comes of it."

"It'll be on your head, then. You always did think you knew everything." Clint turned to stomp out of the room.

King stared after him. *It would be easy to think he's still afraid of something. Maybe he's afraid Dad will talk to me,* he thought.

His father's door stood open. King stepped inside and stopped, shocked by the sight of the figure in the chair. His father stared into the empty fireplace. His face and form appeared much the same except for his extreme thinness. He looked old—a shadow of the vigorous figure of authority King had respected.

"Dad? It's King, Dad. I'm home."

Lambert Sutherland didn't move. King worked his way around in front of the chair and stood facing his father, "I've come home, Dad."

The old man still didn't move, but King saw his eyes gleam with recognition.

Lambert Sutherland's face suddenly contorted in something like a smile and quickly crumpled into tears. The sight of his father crying seemed more than King could bear. He slipped down to his knees and took his father's hands.

"Please don't cry, Dad, please." His father's hands gripped his. King worked one hand free and reached up to wipe the tears from his wrinkled cheeks.

"My horses." Lambert's Sutherland strained to speak. His voice was a croak; his eyes appealed for King's help.

"Don't you worry about the horses. I'll get them back, or I'll get us new ones. I have a plan to put the ranch back on its feet, Dad. I'm going to drive cattle north to the railroad. We've got enough of those ornery black Mexican cows to make us rich."

King could see forgiveness and welcome in his father's eyes. He rose to his feet, pulling his hand out of his father's. "You rest now, Dad. I'm going to take a look around and find out what our men say about this. I'll see you again later on today."

King left his father's room and walked directly to the bench in the courtyard to sit down. He placed both hands between his knees to stop their shaking. The pitiful wreck of a man his father had become tore at his heart.

So much has happened in the last few days that I feel almost crazy, he thought. *I've got to get off by myself and try to clear my head. I can't help myself or anyone else in this state.*

King almost ran out through the back gate of the court-yard and down toward the corrals. The ranch house stood on the crest of a long slope that ended in the canebrakes of a large creek. Patches of trees and brush dotted the plain. The brush got heavier and thicker until it blended into a gray-green mass of willows along the creek banks. There were small groups of cattle grazing here and there. The herd of horses wasn't in sight.

King skirted the bunkhouse, walking quietly. He wanted to avoid meeting anyone else until he could straighten every-thing out in his mind.

"Hey, King." Jeff hailed him as he came in sight of the corral. He was brushing Ranger's sides and the horse was standing like a lamb.

"I should have known that big put-on of a horse would take to you," King said and laughed aloud. "You and Luke Wilson always could charm any horse."

"Aw, he's got plenty of fire, that's a fact, but he shore ain't no fool either. He some-kinda likes this."

"I need a mount, Jeff."

"Take Blaze over there," Jeff motioned toward a shaggy sorrel standing in the corral. "He ain't been rode in a few days, it'd do him good."

King threw his saddle over the sorrel's back and climbed aboard. "Tell them at the house that I'll be back about sundown."

Jeff waved his hand and went back to brushing Ranger.

King let the horse have his head and he lunged out of the corral and galloped across a nearby hill. After a few miles of hard running, King pulled him to a trot.

"I don't think I want to leave home again right away, horse," he said aloud.

He saw more and more small groups of cattle as he guid-ed the horse to lower ground. The grazing improved in that area and hundreds of wild cattle were in view. It would take a force of twenty riders several years to round up all the cat-tle on the ranch. His idea to repair the fortunes of his fami-ly by trailing herds north would surely work.

King pulled the horse sharply to the north to avoid the Mexican village just ahead. The little white stone and adobe houses were clustered around another spring in a grove of trees that nestled against a hill. Several families had lived in the village when Lambert Sutherland bought Blanco Sol. Men and women from the village now worked for the ranch and in the house. The *vaqueros* Juan and Eduardo Valesquez lived there. Their parents, Benito and Elena, worked in the house. Their daughter Rosita was Katherine's maid.

Once behind the crest of the hill, King drew the horse in and dismounted. He felt calmer now. He dropped the reins and walked over to sit on the ground with his back propped against a boulder. He rolled a cigarette and shook his head as he thought over the problems he faced.

Clint stood accused of robbery and murder. His father was speechless and weak, tied to a chair. The ranch had no cash income. Everybody in Texas seemed to be broke. Worse yet, Mercedes seemed determined to make trouble of some sort. He couldn't figure out where to start to help his family. He could only watch and wait at this point—keep his eyes and ears open and be ready. Something would come out that would give him an opening. Then he would know what to do.

King stood up and stretched. Shadows were beginning to lengthen and the air felt cool with the coming of night. He caught up the reins of the horse and mounted, starting back toward the house. It was almost dark when he reached the corrals. Lights shone from the bunkhouse windows. King led Blaze into the corral and unsaddled him. He slapped the horse on his rump and sent him pounding along the fence.

As he pulled the last pole through to close the gate, he saw a slim white form standing in the shadows beside the corral.

"Mercedes?" He knew she would try to waylay him. She certainly didn't believe in wasting time. *I might as well get it over with*, he thought.

King strode closer to the girl and demanded, "What do you want?" He stopped in astonishment when a soft drawling voice that was definitely not Mercedes' answered him.

"As I wasn't looking for you, I don't want anything, Mr. Jonathan Kingsley Sutherland."

King stepped closer still and peered into the girl's face. Shocked and confused, he burst out, "You're not Mercedes."

"I'm well aware of that," the girl said with a delicious giggle.

"Who in the heck are you, then?" King almost yelled in astonishment.

"I'm Sue Ellen Shepherd, your mother's cousin." She looked up at him calmly. Her eyes looked huge and dark in her white face. There was a tiny smile on her well-shaped lips. "I came here to stay when Vicksburg fell."

"You certainly are a surprise. Nobody thought to mention that I even had a beautiful cousin." King finally remembered to remove his hat and bowed.

"You needn't bother yourself to charm me. I've been warned. Besides, I'm certainly not a close enough cousin for you to bother about. My mother's sister was married to your mother's brother. That makes it a pretty long stretch for you to call me cousin."

King's eyebrows shot up at the sarcasm in her lovely voice, but he didn't reply as he continued to examine her. She was an extraordinarily lovely girl. Her dark hair was bound up in a twisted loop at the nape of her slim neck. Her dress appeared almost prim with its high collar and long sleeves, but it fitted her shapely body perfectly. He decided to ignore her tone.

"Are you ready to walk up to the house?" he asked, offering his arm.

Sue Ellen accepted his arm without speaking and walked along beside him, matching her steps to his, not saying a word.

As they passed the bench in the courtyard, King stopped and turned to face her.

"Sit here with me a moment, please, Sue Ellen? There are some things I need to know and you may be able to help me."

She hesitated, glancing up at his face. The sound of his voice and his serious expression seemed to reach her.

Wordlessly, she disengaged her arm and went over to sit on the bench. King sat beside her and thought for a moment. If she had been at the ranch long she had seen and heard things. She might be far enough outside the situation to help. Sue Ellen touched his arm. "You wanted to ask me something? The supper bell will be ringing in a moment."

King turned to face her. Her hand seemed to burn through his sleeve. He was impressed again by her aloof expression and her beauty. Somebody had been telling her wild tales about him, he felt sure. It was probably Mercedes.

"How long have you been staying here?"

"It's around three years now. Why?"

"Please don't get on the defensive." He held up one hand. "My family's in trouble and I need to know what's been happening here for the last year or more. Will you help me?"

"I must tell you I'm glad to see you're finally interested," she stated forcefully.

"Did you think I wouldn't be?"

"What I've heard of you from Clint and Mercedes hasn't made you seem at all interested in your family's problems before the war, maybe not in anything serious. Except running away to help the Yankee army ruin the South."

"I'm thirty-two years old now. That makes me a far different man than I was when I left here more than five years ago—and please remember, the war is over."

Sue Ellen dropped her eyes and answered softly. "Of course you would be different now, forgive me. My father was killed at Vicksburg. It just all came rushing back today when Cousin Katherine told me you were here."

"I'm sorry about your father." King lay his hand over hers. "I wasn't at Vicksburg and I fought for what I believed in, just as he did."

She stared up into his eyes, apparently fighting for control of her emotions. Her nearness made it hard to breathe. King could smell honeysuckle. Pulling his eyes away from hers, he asked, "Please tell me what's been going on around here. I have to know more to help Clint. You're bound to be able to tell me things."

"You know that he's involved with that outlaw Hank Billings and that wretched Spaniard Don Alvaraz?"

"I heard that from an old friend before I even reached San Antonio. It's been about to drive me crazy. Do you think Clint could rob and burn stages and wagons and shoot innocent women and children?"

"No. I do not. I'll never believe that. Clint is sweet and kind, if he is weak. I think Alvaraz and Billings are doing that and that they started the whispering about Clint to cover their own evil doings."

"It's no longer just whispering. They were fairly shouting it out in San Antonio."

"I think I know what's going on. Alvaraz and Billings have some sort of hold on Clint. They made a deal to steal your father's horses and drive them across the border. Alvaraz and the Billings gang made the drive. Clint and Hank stayed at the ranch to make it look as though they were innocent.

"Clint and Hank made a big show of tracking the horses later, but I'm convinced it was just a ruse. They claimed they were driven off the trail by an ambush down close to the border. I was passing Clint's door one day and heard that low-down Mexican woman he's married to screaming at him. I couldn't help but overhear what they were saying. She told the whole story of how they pretended to try to get the horses back."

King was shocked at the disgust in the girl's voice. "Mercedes isn't a Mexican, she's Spanish."

"She—she's—something I can't say." Sue Ellen jumped up. "She said you'd defend her. She claims you'll be lovers again like you were before you left."

"Calm down, girl. That's crazy. I'd never touch Clint's wife, no matter what she'd been to me before they married."

King stood to face Sue Ellen. Her face and eyes were filled with contempt. He was amazed at how much it bothered him for this girl to have such a low opinion of him. As he started to speak again, she turned and ran into the house.

He stood there and watched her, his hands on his hips. He

wanted to call her back, to stay close to her. She was a real spitfire. *Mercedes doesn't have a thing on her for temper.*

When King entered the dining room, the table was covered in bowls and platters of food. Hard times hadn't changed his mother's ways in that respect. He took his place on his mother's left. Mercedes and Clint were seated directly across from him, and Sue Ellen's seat happened to be next to him on his left. She appeared perfectly calm and unruffled, and ignored King completely.

"Have you been introduced to Sue Ellen, dear?" Katherine asked.

"We met out at the corral when I put my horse away earlier. We sort of introduced ourselves, Mother. I am, of course, honored to meet her." He smiled at Sue Ellen.

Sue Ellen looked right back into his eyes and said, "Cousin Katherine, I am delighted to meet your son. He's exactly as I've been told he would be." Her eyes sparkled. King's heart pounded until she looked down at her plate.

"Oh, I'm glad. He was a fine boy when he left, but he's a man now. He has the same look of strength and authority as his father. I do hope you two will get on."

"You can be sure we will, Mother." King grinned down at Sue Ellen as he reached for a bowl of pickled peaches sitting in front of her plate. "We will."

Sue Ellen kept her eyes averted from King throughout the rest of the meal. She joined the general talk but didn't address any remarks directly to him.

King noticed that Mercedes kept her head down and only picked at her food.

"Juan said he saw you riding Blaze out at Willow Spring today," Clint said.

"Yes, I rode out that way. I needed to blow away some cobwebs. A good hard ride always does the trick."

King could see questions in Clint's eyes. He looked to be wondering what King knew and what he thought. *Well, let him wonder,* King thought. *If he gets good and nervous it will be easier for me to get the truth out of him.*

After supper King walked his mother to her door. "It's so

wonderful to have you back, son," Katherine said, holding his hand in both of hers. "I've been afraid since your father's stroke, more afraid than I can say."

"You don't have to be afraid of anything now, Mother. Clint and I will have things humming again before you know it."

"Clint drinks too much. He thinks he hides it from me, but I see more than people think. Mercedes is no wife for him. She rides almost every day and stays out for hours. I believe his worry over what she might be doing, or worse, who she might be meeting, is what is making him drink so much."

"I'll straighten Clint out. He always would listen to me, remember? Don't you worry anymore." He leaned over to kiss her cheek. "Oh, here's something great to think about as you go to sleep. Dad spoke to me."

"You can't mean it. Oh, King, when? What did he say?"

Laughing, he hugged her and kissed her again. It was great to see her happiness. "Dad said, 'my horses' as plain as I'm speaking to you. I honestly believe he'll be all right now. You and Sue Ellen just talk to him all you can. I think he'll start answering you."

"It was the horses being stolen that caused the stroke. He was fine until Clint and that Hank Billings came back from trying to track the rustlers that night. They went into his office and a little later Clint came running out to tell me that your father was ill."

"We'll work it out now, you'll see. Go to sleep. I'll see you in the morning."

Exhausted, King crawled into his bed, his mind a muddle of conflicting thoughts. He tossed and turned, formulating plans and solutions, only to discard them as useless. He finally decided that he had only one real problem and it was Clint's involvement with Alvaraz and Billings.

I only have to watch and wait. When I know enough, I'll brace Clint and get him out of this somehow. Finally satisfied, he relaxed and slipped off to sleep, dreaming of Sue Ellen.

* * *

The next few days King made the rounds of the ranch. Sometimes Clint rode with him. They talked of old times or ranch problems. Every time King tried to turn the conversation to anything close to Clint, he would deftly change the subject. King still believed they would slip back into their old relationship soon and Clint would confide in him.

They were riding south toward the river one morning when King noticed a cloud of dust in the distance. "Look there, Clint, what could that be? Indians never come this close to the house."

Clint looked uncomfortable. "They could though," he said hastily. "There's certainly nothing to stop them."

"Let's ride over that way and take a look." King bent to loosen his rifle in its sheath.

"I'd say we ought to head back closer to the ranch buildings. We couldn't face that many Indians out here in the open." Clint drew his horse to a stop; his voice was getting louder.

"What's the matter with you?" King demanded. "That's the first time I've ever seen you show yellow at a little bunch of Indians."

Clint winced and hung his head.

"Those fellows don't ride like Indians." King shielded his eyes with one hand as he watched. The group of around ten riders was coming up fast. "That fella in front on the black rides like Alvaraz."

The riders were all superbly mounted on dark horses. As they came closer King could see that they wore heavy jackets and gloves. Their legs were covered with leather chaps that showed rough wear. It appeared they had recently been through the desert, where the Cholla cactus hampered travel.

Clint moved his horse close to King's. "Don't cross Alvaraz, King. Please. Just be easy. I can handle him."

King turned to look into Clint's white face. "I ought to run him off the place. You know he claims Blanco Sol rightfully belongs to his family."

"Please," Clint pleaded. "Please don't start anything. Those men will shoot you down and enjoy it."

"All right, boy, it's your play. But you've got some tall explaining to do when we get home."

"Señor King, it is good to see you back from the grave," Alvaraz said as he urged his dancing horse close to King and offered his hand.

King shook the Spaniard's hand and said, "Thanks, Don Alvaraz, it's good to be home."

"My daughter broke her heart when she thought you were lost in the war. She could only be consoled by marriage to your brother." Alvaraz grinned. His yellow teeth gleamed.

King watched Alvaraz's face. *He looks like a wolf,* he thought. *I wonder why he's trying to sound so all-fired nice and friendly.*

"Buenos, Señor Clint." Alvaraz's voice was like silk. He made no effort to lower his tone as he said, "I expected you to visit with me last evening."

"I'll ride over to Riza tomorrow. You don't have to come looking for me." Clint's face flushed red. King could barely hear his whisper.

King recognized several of the riders. Langley Taylor, a rider with a bad name for fighting on both sides of the border, nodded to him. Dale Billings and Jack Thorn sat on their horses and tried not to look straight at him. King wondered why Dale's brother Hank wasn't with them. The other riders were strangers to King, but they had the same hard eyes and brutish expressions as the men he recognized.

Jack Thorn rode a huge bay stallion King recognized with shock as one of his father's horses. He had to struggle to keep his mouth shut as he had promised Clint. It would be out and out foolish for him to start anything with ten gunmen in front of him. King knew he could hold his own with a six-gun against any man, but it was plain that no one would get a fair break with these hardcases.

Alvaraz took Clint to one side and they whispered earnestly. King couldn't hear the words, but Clint seemed to be disagreeing with Alvaraz over something. Finally, Clint yanked his horse away from Alvaraz and called to King. "Let's ride, brother." He struck his horse and pounded off.

"Your brother is nervous. He should learn not to let whiskey master him." Alvaraz said, guiding his horse close to King's again.

King looked at Alvaraz a long time before answering. "Clint hasn't been drinking nearly so much since I came home, and he's been sleeping well every night."

There was no change in Alvaraz's expression. He was quiet for a moment, as though trying to find a hidden meaning in King's statement. "Well, good fortune to him. Whiskey and no sleep will ruin a man. I must ride, Señor King. We will meet again. Adios."

Waving his arm for his men to follow, Alvaraz whirled his horse, pulling cruelly on the Spanish bit to make him rear showily, and then thundered off to the northwest. King followed Clint home. He meant to corner him and get at the truth if he had to beat it out of him.

Clint kept out of his way the next two days, but Mercedes was suddenly right beside King everywhere he turned. He couldn't get away from her. She was completely over her temper fit and was determined to be friendly.

"Come and ride with me today, King," Mercedes called to him as he came out of his room.

"I haven't had my breakfast yet."

"Oh, you lazy, big, lay-abed. I'll wait for you," she said with a gay laugh.

"No, Mercedes, you go on ahead. I want to talk to Clint."

"Pooh, that's no good. He's drunk and hiding in his room. He cannot face you that he took me from you."

"You never were mine and you know it, Mercedes. You never loved me any more than you love Clint. You married Clint. I told you before, that's the end of it for me."

Mercedes moved up close to King and placed one little hand on his chest. "I belonged to you, King Sutherland. I can again. Your brother is a dead man. I won't be his wife for long."

"Get away from me," King whispered, "you poor excuse for a woman. I wouldn't have you anyway."

Suddenly Mercedes placed both hands behind his head and leaped up to kiss his mouth. He yanked himself back from her embrace and pushed her away. A movement caught his eye. He glanced to his left to see Sue Ellen's shocked face across the courtyard.

King reached out with his right hand and shoved Mercedes away from him. "Don't do that again, you crazy fool. I mean it." Shaking with anger, he ran out of the courtyard toward the stables.

Juan was standing beside the bunkhouse holding Mercedes' saddled horse.

"Get me a horse, Juan, fast."

"You will be riding with Señor Clint's wife? No?"

Angrier than ever, King turned toward Juan with his hand over his gun. "What do you mean by that?" he asked menacingly.

"Nothing, Señor King, nothing." The *vaquero* drew back, his mouth open in fear and surprise.

King stared into Juan's face for a moment, then relaxed, realizing the man had no idea how he had angered him. "Forget the horse, Juan. I don't need him now." He turned and strode back through the courtyard, past the hysterically sobbing Mercedes sitting on the stones. She was holding her hand up to hide her face.

Elena stepped back to let King pass through the kitchen door. Her eyes were big with wonder.

"Stop looking at me like that and fix me some breakfast. The sideshow is over."

"Oh no, Señor King." Elena smiled broadly. "The young señora is not finish."

"Stop your gloating, Elena. That was lowdown of me. I simply lost my temper. It's sort of lowdown for you to get so much enjoyment out of it."

"Miss Sue Ellen missed seeing the most important part. She run through here crying at the same time you were pushing that daughter of a pig."

"Elena. Don't be disrespectful."

"Señor King, Mercedes Alvaraz knew the señorita stood in my door when she kiss you."

"Will you let it be, Elena?" King demanded.

The housekeeper scurried to the stove to prepare the food. King went into the dining room and threw himself down in a chair, asking the empty room, "What in the world's going to happen next?"

Chapter Four

King quickly formed a habit of visiting with his father every morning. He sat by his father's chair and told him about what he did in Washington City right after the war. He related how he came to be leading a squad doing crowd control when a young soldier went berserk and rode over him, swinging his saber; how he ended up with a broken leg and the injury that put him out of his head for months.

Lambert Sutherland nodded and occasionally said yes or no. He chuckled out loud when King told him about the advances of the lovely widow he'd roomed with in New Orleans.

King lingered longer than usual this morning. His mind was on the fiasco with Mercedes in the courtyard. The sun was high when he went outside. As soon as he stepped into the courtyard he saw Sue Ellen sewing in the shade of the porch near the kitchen door. He crossed over to stand before her.

"Sue Ellen, can I talk to you?" His voice sounded strange to his ears. He felt guilty and confused about his feelings for her and sick that she should have seen Mercedes kiss him.

Sue Ellen stood up. "I have some things to do right now, please excuse me." Her voice was cold and she kept her face turned away from him.

"Hold on, now, girl. That's not fair." King reached out to

touch her arm. He felt compelled to make her understand, to make her want to look at him again.

Jerking her arm away from his hand, Sue Ellen turned on him with blazing eyes. "Not fair? You're a fine one to talk about fairness."

"You could at least hear me out. I can explain what happened between Mercedes and me yesterday."

"Please don't even try. You're a cad. It's that simple, and it's the only possible explanation for your conduct. Let me pass."

As she started around him, King reached out and grabbed her shoulders with both hands. "Not until you listen. I'll explain and then I'll want to know why you're so all-fired upset by Mercedes kissing me. I'm getting confusing signals here."

"Upset! Any decent person would be upset by such goings on. You are a disgrace." Sue Ellen almost hissed the words and her beautiful face turned fiery red.

"That kiss was none of my doing. You shouldn't make up your mind without hearing what really happened."

"Take your filthy hands off me." She shook her shoulders and tried to pull away from his hands.

King tightened his grip and shook her hard. "Well if you won't listen, think this over." He pulled her close to him. Dropping his head, he kissed her on the lips.

Sue Ellen's eyes opened wide in shock. She hit out at King with her fists. He released her and stepped back. "You're reading me all wrong, Sue Ellen," he said, then turned and almost ran away from the porch, leaving her standing there, still staring and holding both hands against her burning cheeks.

King's lips burned where they had touched Sue Ellen's. He stopped outside the courtyard to catch his breath, cursing himself for a fool. He wanted her, had wanted her from first sight, but everything he did seemed to make her hate him.

The Hastings brothers arrived early that morning. The Mexican guide, Juan Marcel, was on horseback, riding ahead of the wagon. The brothers shouted greetings from the seat and the wagon body.

"We finally made it, King," said Neale. He was covered with trail dust and there was a heavy growth of sandy beard on his face.

"We never woulda got here without Juan's help, but here we are."

"Jump down and come on in the bunkhouse, boys. I had begun to think you were lost somewhere." King felt reassured at the sight of the young men. They leaped down from the wagon, seeming glad to stretch their bodies and feel their strength.

King felt a lift of happiness and hope as he led the group of men into the bunkhouse. "There's bunks enough for everybody. Just pick out one of those with the mattress all rolled up. There's a big cabin on that hill above the house you can live in later. It'll take some work to make it fit to live in first, so make yourselves comfortable here for a few days. Some of the boys will show you around."

King left the Hastings brothers to settle in and walked back up to the house. He had made up his mind to face Clint and make him tell his story. He tapped on Clint's door and called out, "Open up. We've got things to talk about."

There was no answer. He rattled the door. It wasn't latched. Opening it, he quickly stepped inside and closed it, leaning back against the panels.

"Clint, wake up." He could see his brother's form under the quilts. He walked over to stand by the bed and look down at him.

"Get up, you lump. You've avoided me all you're going to."

Clint groaned and slid further down into the bed, his face hidden. King grabbed the covers and yanked them off the bed, tossing them on the floor.

Furious, Clint jumped up from the bed to face King. His baggy gray long johns and bare feet made him look ridiculous.

"Get the devil out of here!" he yelled. "You have no right to barge in here and pull me out of my bed."

"I have every right, you lily-livered weasel," King yelled

back. "Put on your pants, doggone your time, and start talking."

Clint flopped back down on the bed and covered his face with his hands. "Please, King," he begged, with pain in his voice. "I've always loved you. You'll hate me for sure if I tell you the truth."

"I almost hate you now, you miserable skunk. Stop feeling sorry for yourself and level with me. I can't help you if you won't tell me anything."

"I can't tell you and nobody can help me."

Clint was almost crying. He stood up shakily and pulled on his pants. He picked up a pair of socks from the floor and yanked them up on his feet, then sat down on the bed and pulled on his boots.

"I wish to heck you'd stayed in Washington City," he muttered.

"Aw, Clint. Stop this. You're acting like you did when you were ten years old and got yourself in Dutch with the old man with some of your foolishness."

"I tell you, King, it's no use, you can't help me. You can only get yourself killed if you try to mix in this."

"I'm not going to get killed. I'm going to do some killing. I'm thinking I'll take Billings and Alvaraz for starters."

Clint jumped at King's words. "You'll never get a chance. I know you're good enough to outdraw either one of them in a fair fight, but they don't fight fair."

"Just tell me what they've got on you." King turned a chair around and sat down facing his brother.

Clint ran his hand over the thin stubble on his face. His eyes looked hollow and haunted. It made King's heart ache to watch him.

"They've got too much on me for you to ever do anything about it. Those dirty devils have made my name a horror story. Mother would die of shame if she knew what they've been saying about me."

"She'll find out for sure if we don't put a stop to this thing. Mother's not stupid. She just lives in a world of her own, with

Dad at the center of it. Mercedes is threatening to tell her everything. You can depend on her doing that eventually."

"That cat. I hate her."

"Why in the world did you ever marry her. You sure didn't have to."

Clint looked straight at King. His face was full of shame. "I know that. It had to be part of taking your place here. She was your woman. When Alvaraz got worried that she would completely disgrace him and pushed me into making an honest woman of her, I fell in with it without a whimper. I guess I thought it would make me more like you.

"Mother tried to talk me out of it. She could see that Mercedes wasn't a wife for any man. Dad fairly screamed when he found out what I planned to do. He knew she was a tramp. I got as stubborn as a mule and bone stupid. I wouldn't listen to anyone."

"That's as it might be, but whatever led up to this, she's got to be controlled. You can't do that lying around drunk all the time. Let's stop dancing around what's important here. Tell me the whole story of your involvement with Alvaraz and Billings, Clint. You can't keep hiding. I have to know everything."

Standing up, Clint began to pace the floor. His fists were clenched, his face twisted. He stopped and rolled a cigarette. Finally, leaning against the wall, he began to speak, "I got into trouble first by drinking with the polecats. Alvaraz invited Hank Billings and me to Riza to play cards and he furnished the red-eye.

"Hank and me were trapping wild horses and breaking them for the army. We used some of the Riza *vaqueros* to help in big drives. It made plenty of money, but Dad's income from the ranch had dwindled down to nothing. Everything he had went to the Confederacy. There was no money from the shipping business in Charleston, of course.

"Cattle were worthless and Dad wouldn't sell any of his horses for army use. It takes a lot of money to keep this ranch going even with only three riders. Mother couldn't understand. She's never known what it is not to have money.

"I finally lost so much money to Alvaraz and his bunch by playing cards that I was desperate. He and Hank approached me with the idea of selling some of Dad's horses. I talked to Dad but he wouldn't hear of it. He just assumed that what money I made with the wild horses would be used to run the ranch.

"They led me in deeper and deeper, and fool that I am, I went for it. Then they started pushing me hard to agree to help them drive some of Dad's horses. They finally came up with the idea of making it appear as though Mexican bandits were behind the raid. I still held out. They pushed me harder and harder. Alvaraz finally got Mercedes to start on me. She's as lowdown as he is.

"As you've probably figured out by now, in the end, I agreed to the deal, I'm ashamed to say. They said they were going to cut out about half of the herd and run them to the border. It was easy. We'd never had reason to watch the horses at night, and most of them are like pets. Hank came to the house that night and we sat there in the library pretending to have a friendly game of cards. Juan came running in about dawn, yelling that a bunch of bandits had run off with the herd.

"Hank and I jumped up and lit out as though we were after them. We made Jeff and the *vaqueros* believe they were needed here to protect what was left of the herd. Dad was raring to go until Mercedes claimed she saw a man skulking around the house and got Mother scared. Dad stayed here to protect them.

"Hank and I stayed out for three days. We rode through brush and Cholla cactus to wear out our horses and make it look like we'd been riding hard after the bandits. When we came back in here empty-handed, Dad met us at the gate. He led us into his office and closed the door. He stood and looked at us with that questioning look on his face. I could see that he was suspicious—he always could smell a trick a mile away.

"I told him the story we had agreed on and had a hard time getting the words out. I claimed we had followed the trail to the border and been stopped and turned back by an ambush. That we had barely escaped with our lives. Dad finally said, 'Something's wrong with this whole deal, Clint. You just shut up.'

"He turned to Hank and yelled, 'You know something, you slimy rattlesnake. What's going on here?' Hank just laughed in his face and said, 'Your little sonny boy has really done it this time, old man.'

"Dad jerked all over and lunged for me. He never reached me. The blood drained from his face and he fell to the floor, right there in front of me. He was out cold. I ran for Mother and Hank took off. As you know, Dad hasn't looked at me since. He knows I was in on that deal and it broke him."

King started to speak, but Clint stopped him with a wave of his hand.

"Wait, I haven't told you the half of it. The worst is to come. If I stop talking now, I'll never get it all out."

Clint rolled another cigarette and took a long pull. "Hank slipped back in the house the next night. He acted different. I guess he and Alvaraz figured in together all along. I met him in the hall right beside Mercedes' bedroom.

"He handed me a small bag of coins and said, 'Alvaraz sent this to you on account, Clint. You'll have to take the rest from time to time when we can pay it.' It contained only five hundred dollars. The herd was supposed to bring enough to square me with Alvaraz and set me up for months. I went a little wild. Hank just laughed in my face and said, 'Don't go talking too fast, boy. I just might have to have a talk with your ma.'

"I think I realized then what I had gotten myself into. Alvaraz started sending me a message to ride over to Riza at night to pick up a payment. It happened several times. Later, I rode into San Antonio for supplies and got the shock of my life.

"Everywhere I went I got the cold shoulder. I couldn't figure it out. I finally braced Charlie Davis at the livery stable. He didn't want to say anything. He acted like he didn't even want to be seen speaking to me. When I pushed him to tell me what was the matter with everybody, he finally told me what people were saying.

"He said that wagons and stages were being held up and robbed. The people in them were shot to death and some were even scalped as if by Indians, but some thought it might be the work of a gang of outlaws on shod horses. People were beginning to believe it was the work of a gang of cutthroats and I was part of it. Me!

"Can you believe that, King? People think I'm a lowdown cutthroat robber and murderer of innocent people. There's women and children on those wagon trains and people are saying I'm involved in murdering them."

Clint turned away again to pace up and down. King stayed quiet, sitting still, watching his brother with shock in his eyes.

"I am guilty in a way, King. Alvaraz has been giving me money that came from each robbery—a little from each one—enough to make me as guilty as he is." He sat down on the bed again and watched King's face. He was crying.

King's heart ached for him. *Poor stupid kid, no wonder he's been drinking*, he thought.

It was his turn to jump up to pace the floor. When Clint got control of himself, King walked back over to the bed. "We've got to expose Billings and Alvaraz, Clint. Killing them won't be enough. If you're ever going to be able to hold your head up again, we've got to expose them—to make sure people know the truth."

"If we try anything, they'll tell Mother and Dad," Clint said. "Mercedes knows Dad is better since you came home. Another shock would kill him for sure. Besides, I've been seen out at night every time a stage or wagon train has been attacked. How will I ever explain that I never rode with them on one of those raids?"

"Maybe you won't have to explain. Mercedes knows the details, I'd be willing to bet on that. I'll make her tell the truth."

"That woman wouldn't tell the truth on a stack of Bibles. We're going to have to do better than that."

"Go take a bath and clean yourself up, Clint. I've got to have time to think. There's a way out of this and we're going to find it. Come on outside when you're ready. There's some people I want you to meet."

King left Clint's room. He felt sick at the depths his brother had reached. *At least he's not bad*, he thought. *He's just weak and stupid. I'm thankful for that much.*

When he re-entered the courtyard, the Hastings brothers were standing under the cottonwood beside the spring. He was impressed again by the sight of their handsome, open faces. They were clean-shaven and had slicked their hair back and had on clean clothes.

"You boys sure do look a heck of a lot better than you did when you rode in here a little while ago."

"You bet," said Ben, the youngest. "Neale was sure glad too. There was a mighty pretty lady here by the spring when we walked up."

Neale looked embarrassed.

"Look at his red face," the incorrigible boy said, laughing. "I ain't never seen old Neale so fussed before."

"Oh, shut your big mouth, kid," Neale said.

"I'll shut up, but I'll bet Mr. Sutherland has to run you away from the house with a stick." Ben ducked behind Henry's back to grin at Neale.

King suddenly felt uncomfortable, his chest burning with an irrational anger at Neale Hastings. "Please have a seat, boys," he said tersely. "My brother will be here to meet you in a few minutes."

Sue Ellen emerged from the kitchen door followed by Elena, with a tray laden with glasses and a pitcher of lemonade. "Y'all come here to the table and sit, Mr. Hastings. I'll pour your lemonade while Elena fixes up a meal for you." The Hastings brothers moved as a group to cluster around Sue Ellen. She smiled sweetly as she looked up into Neale's face.

King felt his temper rising. He knew this was her way of getting back at him. He turned away and strode off toward his mother's room. The sound of Sue Ellen's gay laughter over some remark one of the Hastings brothers made followed him.

Katherine sat at a table writing letters. She looked up and smiled as he entered the room. "I thought you were away from the ranch somewhere, son. What's wrong? Why are you angry?"

"Oh, it's nothing. I'm fine. Have you seen Dad this morning?"

"Yes, I have. I spent an hour with him right after you left him. He puzzles me. Sometimes I believe he's angry with me about something."

"What could he be angry with you about?"

"I think it has something to do with Clint. I talk about everything I can think of to him. He's been following everything I say with interest since you came home. He even gets out a word now and then, but whenever I mention Clint, his face just closes up and he turns away. Nothing I can say will make him look at me again."

"He couldn't be angry with you, Mother. He probably knows more about what's going on than we think. Maybe it's because of Clint's drinking." King trembled with fear for his mother. She should never have to bear knowing what Clint had gotten himself involved in.

"I came in here to tell you that some people arrived that I met on the boat from New Orleans. These men were in need of a job so I sent them cross-country by wagon with a guide. I thought they could live in the old trapper's cabin after we fix it up a little. They're five brothers from Tennessee. A family named Hastings. They lost everything in the war and are trying to make a new life here."

Katherine reached out to lay one hand on King's cheek. "You're a good man, King. I'm proud of you."

King took her hand in his and kissed it. "No, I didn't ask them here to be good to them. They're going to learn to punch cattle."

"American men as riders? Are you sure? We've always had trouble with them in the past."

"These men are different. They want a new life and a

chance to build something. You should hear their story. They had to sell their horses and walk to get as far as New Orleans. They stayed together and worked for two years to get enough money to get them all to Galveston on the packet boat. They were almost flat broke when they got on that boat, trusting that they would be able to find work in Texas so they could make a new life."

"They certainly sound different from the other American riders we've had. I should go out and greet them."

"Sue Ellen is taking care of the hospitality for you, Mother, and she seems to be enjoying it greatly."

Katherine caught his eyes with hers. "Son, she's a beautiful young woman at the right age for a husband. If these men are as fine as you say they are, what could be the objection? There certainly aren't many men to choose from around here."

"Husband!" King burst out, almost shouting in surprise and shock. He stared at his mother's expressionless face for a moment before he turned and walked out of the room without another word.

King rode Ranger the rest of the day. He went far afield, within sight of the furthermost line camp. He stopped and gazed, leaning his arms on the pommel of his saddle. His mind simply didn't want to work, his thoughts were all in a tangle. He worried about Clint and Mercedes and his father and mother. But every time he tried to concentrate on finding a solution to their problems, Sue Ellen Shepherd's beautiful face popped up. He saw her looking up at Neale Hastings with that sweet smile on her face. *I'll be no good to Clint or anybody else if I can't get her out of my head*, he thought.

He finally gave up trying to think and turned back toward the ranch. When he spurred Ranger, the big horse responded like he was fresh, fairly leaping into a swinging run. King found he had to concentrate on his riding.

It was dark when King entered the courtyard gate. He wandered under the cottonwood and leaned against its trunk to roll a cigarette. He heard a soft sound from the kitchen door. He peered through the darkness, but could see nothing. As he neared the door, he could hear the sound better. Someone was crying. A little form was huddled on the kitchen step. He could see her in the light from the kitchen. It was Rosita, Elena's daughter.

King stepped nearer and whispered, "Rosita. What's wrong? Why are you crying like this?"

Rosita raised her head. Tears covered her face. Her eyes were red and swollen. "Oh, Señor King," she said, and dropped her head to begin sobbing again.

King took her hand and patted it, kneeling down on the flagstones beside her. "There now, little one, you stop this crying and tell me."

"I cannot tell you, Señor King. I must not." The girl wiped her eyes and, taking the handkerchief King held out, blew her nose. Her black eyes were tragic. "The señora would kill me."

"What have you done?" King asked gently.

The girl was completely distraught. Her hands clutched nervously at her blouse. She huddled in the doorway as though she could hide there.

"Come on now, Rosita. You've been my little girl since you were a baby. You've grown up some since I've been away, but you can still cry on my shoulder." King leaned close to her face and smiled to reassure her.

"I am *embarazada*. I am to have a child," she whispered.

King stared at her, and said dryly, "Boy, have you ever grown up."

"It is your brother's child."

"Clint! Well, blast his hide anyway. What's he going to do next?" King slammed one fist into his outstretched hand. For an instant he almost hated Clint. He jumped to his feet.

"No, señor, no. It is not your brother's fault. It was my doing. I have always loved him. When he married I tried to keep away, but he is so unhappy and I am not good."

"Hush, Rosita, of course you're good. Clint should be horsewhipped. Even if he is unhappy, that's no excuse for him to touch you."

"I let him touch me. I ask him to touch me. He would have avoided me, but I meet him when he comes home late at night. It is all my fault."

"Rosita, what are you planning to do? When is the baby to come?"

"It is many months. I will go away soon so she will not find out."

"Does my mother know, Rosita? She would help you."

"No. No. The señora has such a heavy load to bear. She should not know. I do not want her to know."

"I thought you meant you didn't want Mercedes to know you were carrying Clint's child."

"That dirty liar. If she had a baby that Hank Billings would be its father. I would be proud to tell her I will have her husband's child."

"What are you saying, girl—Mercedes and Hank Billings? How do you know this?"

"I see them together. Juan and Eduardo see them too. She meets him almost every day. She rides out of sight of the ranch and circles around to the back of the old cabin. Hank Billings, he meets her there. They stay inside the cabin for hours. They have blankets on the floor for a bed."

King remembered Mercedes trying to get him to ride with her. He wondered if Billings had been meeting her that day. *They may have been planning a party with me as the guest of honor*, he thought angrily.

"I'll take care of Hank Billings, Rosita, but what can I do to help you?"

"I will be all right, Señor King. I promise you. Please keep my secret?"

"It's a secret that can't be kept, child. You know that. Why, your mother probably knew before you did."

"Oh, *por Dios*. You are right." Rosita started crying anew. King sat beside her and held her slight shoulders in his arms as she sobbed.

"Stop that crying now. Go inside and sleep. I'll figure out what to do. I'll help you when the time comes."

"Clint would help if he knew."

"You mean you haven't told him? For heaven's sake, Rosita, he deserves to know. He deserves to worry some too."

"Please do not tell him. You must promise me you will not tell him."

"I'll not tell him yet, but one of us will have to sooner or later. You go inside now." King turned away from the girl and walked back over to the spring, sitting down heavily on the stone bench.

He burned with anger that Billings would meet Clint's wife within sight of the ranch house. *That miserable nervy coyote will find out where trouble started*, he thought. King's hand dropped to his Colt. His fingers curled around the grip. It had been years since he had drawn his gun on a man. His great speed and deadly accuracy with a pistol had been respected once.

He never stopped practicing. His hand was supple and smooth. Billings would never outdraw him if he could force him to fight. If he could down Billings in a fair fight, it would make it easier to get to Alvaraz and it would take some attention off Clint.

For some days later, King rose early each morning, but Mercedes didn't go riding. Clint went out with the Hastings brothers every day. The men were eager and learned by doing. With the help of the *vaqueros* they searched the brakes of the creek and river for cattle and put the Sutherland circle star brand on their flanks.

As the days passed, it was good for King to see the change in Clint. He was eating better. Long hours in the saddle tanned his face and the marks of dissipation that had scarred it began to disappear.

King began to feel impatient for something to break. The Quivira boys and Luke would be riding in soon and he wanted them to stay. If he couldn't get Clint clear of Alvaraz, they would ride on and he couldn't blame them if they did. No cowhand could survive a bad name. It would drive him down to stealing to eat. Then he would have to kill to protect himself. It would only be a matter time before a gun or rope would end his life.

It was almost a week before King saw Mercedes come out of her room early one morning. She ran across the courtyard dressed in riding clothes. He jumped up from his seat by his father's chair and ran out to stop at the gate and watch her ride off. She headed downhill, away from the cabin. King decided to sneak around from the other side. He could slip up near the cabin before she got there.

King hurried to get Ranger ready. He rode in a wide circle north of the house and tied Ranger in some brush well away from the cabin.

"Stand easy, boy. I'll be back soon enough," he said, patting the horse on his shoulder.

He crept up close to the blind side of the cabin. A horse stood tied almost out of his line of sight against the porch. It was one of his father's Durango whites. King shook his head in astonishment. It was an incredible break. The horse itself gave him reason enough to shoot Billings without confronting him. King's thoughts became grim and controlled. This was going to be simple. Billings obviously felt overconfident or the horse would be hidden more carefully.

King stood with his back to the cabin wall and waited. Minutes dragged by. Suddenly he heard a step inside the cabin. Billings walked out onto the porch. King heard him walk over and stop at the step. Mercedes came riding up the trail, her horse at a gallop. She stopped in the yard and dismounted.

"Have you seen anyone around here this morning?" she called out to Billings as she walked toward the cabin.

"Of course not, baby," Billings answered. "Nobody ever comes here."

"They will be coming now. They are going to fix this cabin up for some farmers King brought out from Galveston." Mercedes step sounded on the porch.

"We'll have to find us some other place to meet, sugar."

"I think we should stop meeting for a while, Hank. Something is going on. Clint has stopped drinking and I think King is watching me. I believe Clint told him something that has him suspicious."

Billings laughed and said, "Stop worrying yore pretty head about it. That pore husband of yours is too yella to tell King Sutherland what he's got hisself into. King would kill him. Stop all this talking and let's go inside before the day is plumb over."

King heard a muffled sound from Mercedes. He stepped around the corner of the cabin and said, "Draw your gun, Billings."

Hank Billings pushed Mercedes out of his arms with his left hand and turned to face King. "I ain't got no quarrel with you, King." His face blanched.

"The devil you say." King stood still, his left hand held out over his gun. "Stop talking and fill your hand, you miserable skunk."

Billings tried to laugh. "You shore are almighty fussed about me meeting yore brother's wife. Shore it ain't something personal?"

King's whole body jumped with anger. His hand fell closer to his gun. His long fingers trembled. "Draw your gun, you sorry horse thief, or I'll shoot you down like a dog."

"Leave him alone, King," screamed Mercedes. "He cannot outdraw you. If you kill him I will talk."

King laughed out loud, never taking his eyes from Billings' face. "Go ahead and talk. You've made sure by your actions that nobody's going to believe anything you say."

At King's words, Billings lunged for his gun. It was still in his holster when he fell. King's bullet left a blue hole in the middle of his forehead. As his body sagged to the porch floor, Mercedes fell to her knees beside him, shrieking.

King walked around to the front and stepped up on the porch. He reached over and grabbed Mercedes' arm to pull her roughly to her feet. "You get out of here right now. If I ever see you again, I'll shoot you, even if you are a woman."

"You'll pay for this, King Sutherland. I'll make sure you pay." Her face contorted with grief and hate, Mercedes leaped for King. Her hands were claws, reaching for his face. He caught her arms and held her helpless.

"I meant what I said, Mercedes. I know everything. Go tell your father Hank Billings is dead and that I said he's next."

"You talk big, but you are only one man. My father has many men."

"I can get help. Tell your father that."

"Go rot, you murderer." Still crying, Mercedes stalked off to mount her horse. She whipped him to a hard gallop as she rode toward the Alvaraz ranch.

King left the body of Hank Billings lying on the cabin porch. He planned to send Juan or Eduardo and another man to bury him. He untied the white horse and led him close to where he left Ranger. The big black screamed a challenge that the white stallion answered every bit as loudly.

"Here, you two, stop it. Calm down, you ornery studs." Holding Ranger with an iron hand, King led the white horse on a long rope. He had to fight Ranger every step of the way back to the corral.

Jeff ran out of the barn at the sight of King and the horse he was leading. "The Durango! Where'd you get him?" Grabbing the rope from King, he led the horse to a separate corral, a good distance away from Ranger.

"He's a gift from Hank Billings. Jeff, get Juan or Eduardo to take another man and a couple of shovels up to the trapper's cabin and bury Hank. He's lying on the porch."

"Bury him? You shot him?"

"I did and I feel good about it, I'm sorry to say. I gave him an even break, though. I guess the war must have made me harder than I thought."

King dismounted. "Tie Ranger for me, Jeff. Loosen his gear and get him some grain. I'll need him later. Give me a few minutes, then bring that ornery old white horse up to the courtyard. He just might be exactly the medicine Dad needs. He was always one of his favorites."

King found his father in a chair beside the spring.

Walking over to him, King asked, "Do you feel up to a surprise, old man? It's a great one, I promise."

His father nodded. King sat on the ground beside his chair. "Watch the gate, Dad."

A faint smile played across Lambert Sutherland's face. King almost held his breath, watching his father. He could hear the horse coming. His hooves rattled against stone as he approached.

His father's head snapped up as the horse came in sight. "Renato," he whispered.

Jeff led the horse into the courtyard and up close to Sutherland. King watched as his father's hands gripped the arms of his chair. He struggled to stand. King jumped up and took him by one arm to steady him. "It's Renato," his father repeated, reaching out to rub the horse's silky nose.

Renato recognized his master and pushed his nose against his chest, knocking him back down into his chair. Sutherland's great laugh boomed out.

King felt almost giddy with delight. "Oh, Dad. You are happy to have him back, aren't you?" He placed his arm around his father's shoulders and hugged him.

"Yes, son. Yes, I'm happy," Lambert responded.

King could see tears in his father's eyes, and he felt happier than he had in weeks.

Katherine and Sue Ellen came running out of the house. "What's going on here, King?" Katherine asked. "What's Renato doing in my garden?"

"He's making Dad happy, Mother. Come here and look at his face."

Katherine saw the gladness in her husband's eyes and whispered, "Oh, Lambert darling." She held out her hand. Sutherland reached up and accepted it, pulling her down beside him.

"I'm all right now," he said huskily. His words were slow but clear. Katherine dropped her head against his arm and burst into tears.

King turned to Sue Ellen and said, "Let's go for a walk."

She looked at him strangely for a moment, then, ignoring his proffered arm, she walked beside him down to the corral fence.

"Katherine's happy now. Nothing matters to her but your father."

"I know. That's the first sign of affection he's shown her since his stroke." King leaned his arms on the top rail of the fence and stared off toward the creek. "She must have been breaking her heart over it all this time."

He glanced sideways at Sue Ellen's profile. Her closeness made his heart pound. She was as beautiful as a cameo. Her skin was smooth and pale against her dark hair. King saw a tear slide down her cheek. He wanted to touch it, to trace its path down her face to the curve of her mouth.

"King?" Her voice startled him. She turned to face him. "Elena told me what really happened in the courtyard with Mercedes the other day. I'm ashamed of the way I acted toward you afterwards." Her eyes were hidden in her long eyelashes.

"Look at me, Sue Ellen."

A blush stained her cheeks. King didn't touch her. He just waited.

She raised her eyes and looked up at him. Her expression was wary but her eyes were soft and serious. King caught his breath when he looked into them.

"I'm not going to say I'm sorry I kissed you. I'm sorry it happened in anger. I'll ask you to forgive me for that."

"You shouldn't have done it, you know."

"It hit me so hard when I realized how much it meant to me for you to think I'd fool around with Mercedes that I couldn't help myself."

"Please don't touch me again. I'm not one of your dance hall girls." Her voice was firm. The softness had gone out of her eyes. Without waiting for King to answer, she turned and walked quickly back to the house.

Chapter Five

King rode westward toward the place where he and Clint had met Alvaraz and his men earlier. He gave Ranger his head and the horse increased his speed to a full gallop that ate up the miles. King was thinking so hard that he hardly noticed where he rode. When he finally started looking at his surroundings, he realized that bunches of cattle stood under the widespread limbs of nearby live oaks. The new grass grew thick and heavy. Willow thickets filled low spots. Patches of wild cane dotted the area near the river.

The river ran wide and shallow at this point. When he reached an opening in the thick brush, he turned Ranger downhill. Long sandbars jutted into the shallow water. He recognized the crossing. It had been years since he'd been to this spot. If he crossed the river here, he would be only a few miles from Lost Valley.

The valley was a narrow cleft that could easily be missed if you didn't know exactly how to find it. Benito Valesquez had taken him there when he was a boy. They visited it several times on hunting trips. The ride into the valley was easy if you knew the way.

He found horse tracks on the sandbar. Stopping Ranger, he leaned over to study them. They were fresh, maybe one or two days old at the most. It looked like the tracks of six horses. All of them were shod.

The tracks headed away from the river back the way King had just come. This wasn't a regular trail. The country to the south was too broken and rough for riders to come up this way from the Rio Grande. King was puzzled. Why would a group of riders come this way?

He decided to follow their back trail and see if he could find anything. After he crossed the river, the tracks were easy to follow. The riders hadn't made any attempt to hide. Their back trail turned to the west and started up the long hill. He soon realized it was leading directly to the entrance to Lost Valley. King loosened his gun in its holster and pulled Ranger to a walk. The narrow opening was shaded by heavy brush from this direction. The horses' tracks disappeared as they came out on solid rock.

Slipping to the ground, he led Ranger far enough into a group of pines so he couldn't be easily seen and tied him securely. He took an extra box of shells out of his saddlebag and carried his rifle. Stopping to reach down, he removed his spurs and placed them in the saddlebag. They might give him away if someone was in the valley.

He found a lot of old horse signs. A large group of horses had been along the trail some time before, but the new sign showed only a few horses. There had always been wild horses in the area. They came into the valley to water at the springs.

King made his way carefully down the trail, keeping close to the rock wall. The valley opened up quickly; the narrow passage became a wide trail and then a grassy slope. He heard the scream of a stallion. Ranger's answer rang against the hills. King jumped closer against the wall and took cover in a cleft in the rock. The stallion blasted another challenge.

If that doggone horse keeps on, Ranger will come down here after him, King thought.

He could see well down into the valley from his position. A small group of dark-colored horses grazed in plain sight. Ranger finally quieted. King walked carefully down the hill. He rounded a bend in the trail and stopped in astonishment. There was a fence across the opening. Someone had pulled cedars up the slope and piled them across the entrance to the valley.

The last twenty feet or so of the barrier was four strands of heavy wire held up by long cedar poles. Someone had trapped those horses. It must have been wild horse hunters. He wondered if they knew they were on Sutherland range.

When he came up to the wire barrier, King could see the horses clearly. Many were white and most of them were solid in color. *Wild horses would be mixed colors,* King puzzled to himself. *These horses are too big and heavy to be mustangs. There must be thirty or forty solid white ones in that bunch.* With a shock, he realized what had happened. *It's—it's—the Durango whites! Dad's horses!*

King trembled with excitement. For an instant he felt dizzy at his discovery. The horses had been right here for more than a year, within less than a day's ride of the house. And Clint never had never known. He had never even thought about it. He was too busy drinking and wallowing in self-pity.

Turning, King rushed back up the trail to Ranger. Forgetting the possibility that someone might be watching the horses, he ran the last few steps. He returned his rifle to its sheath on the saddle. Quickly replacing his spurs, he mounted and urged the horse to hurry. He held Ranger to a trot until he crossed the river, then let him set the pace. The horse ran for a while, then settled down to a mile-eating canter.

It was late by the time King reached the ranch buildings, but he had made the necessary plans to recover the horses. He knew his tracks would be seen. If he didn't move fast, whoever was holding the horses in the valley would surely move them. The tracks he followed showed that someone had checked on them only a few days earlier.

The ranch boasted nine riders, including Clint. There were Mexican men at the village who would ride with them. It wouldn't be any problem to get the horses back home, but it had to be done quickly. If guards were in the valley, they might have to fight.

One man lay dead already. Others would surely die before this was over. King believed it inevitable that they would face a pitched battle with Alvaraz and his gang. It seemed possible and perhaps probable that Alvaraz would attack the ranch house to avenge Billings. When he knew the horses had been found, Alvaraz would certainly attempt to get them back.

King let Ranger into the corral and walked to the bunk-house. He hit the door with his fist and yelled, "Don't shoot, boys, it's King."

Jeff's feet hit the floor instantly. "What's the matter, King?"

"Make a light, Jeff, and get everybody up. We've got work to do."

Henry and Daniel Hastings were on their feet when Jeff lit the lamp. Neale and Ben climbed down from their top bunks, grumbling sleepily.

"What the devil is all the noise? It's the middle of the night," Neale said.

"Shut up," said Willis Hastings. "It's the boss."

The men gathered around King. "I've found our horses, men, the whole herd. They're about six hours' ride to the west, boxed in a hidden valley. We're going after them at first light. There'll likely be shooting, are you boys game?"

"Shucks, man. Why wait till morning?" Jeff was almost dancing with excitement.

"We're ready. Let's go now." Neale spoke for his brothers, as usual.

"I'll want Neale and Daniel to go. I'll be here at dawn. You boys be armed and ready to ride."

King turned to Jeff. "I know you want to go with us, but we need more men to protect the ranch. Things are going to get rough. You'll have to ride to Santone, starting right now. Lead a spare horse and ride as fast as you can. Find Luke Wilson. Tell him to round up the Quivira bunch and bring all the shells he can carry. I need him fast."

"Willis, you and Henry and Ben bring your rifles to the house at first light tomorrow. I want you to close the gates and stand guard. It'll take us until dawn Wednesday to get back here with the horses if everything goes right. It's a strong possibility that Alvaraz may decide to pay you a visit before we get back. Clint knows enough to hang Alvaraz and the Spaniard's sure to try to kill him. I'm going down to the village to tell Juan and Eduardo about the horses and I'll ask them to get a few more *vaqueros* to ride with us to get them."

"Juan's riding guard on the remuda," Jeff said.

"We'll surely need those horses. I'll send Eduardo after him. I'm going to tell Clint and get a few hours' sleep; you boys do the same."

Jeff left the bunkhouse with King. "Ride carefully, Jeff, but hurry," King told him. "We've got to have some help if Alvaraz attacks us. Tell Luke I need him, fast. He'll come running. Be sure to tell him I said he was wrong about Clint."

"Gosh, boss, that's a real blessing. I was shore scared Clint might be riding with them devils like folks was saying."

"Well, he wasn't. You tell Luke that first thing."

King decided to let Clint sleep. He'd wake him at dawn. If he told him about the horses being at their back door now, he'd be so excited he'd never go back to sleep. He pulled his saddle off Ranger and turned him into the corral. Catching the big sorrel named Blaze by his hackamore, he led him over to the fence and put his saddle and bridle on him. As soon as the horse was ready, he mounted and rode toward the Mexican village.

The dogs barked frantically as he rode between the houses. He pulled the horse up in front of Benito's door as Eduardo stepped out under the trellis. He was completely dressed and held his rifle in his left hand.

"I heard you coming for a mile, *jefe*. Is there more trouble with the horses?"

"Not trouble, Eduardo. I've found the horses Alvaraz stole. Go tell Juan and help him push the remuda along to the corral. We're going after them at dawn."

"Where are the horses?"

"Your father could have found them anytime at all if he hadn't gotten too old and fat to do any hunting."

"They were in the Lost Valley! Why would they be there, *jefe*?"

"I've been asking myself that question for hours. I can't figure it out. Get some of your amigos to ride with us. Make sure they're men you can trust. There's plenty of time for someone to ride to Riza and warn Alvaraz if they were of a mind to do such a thing."

"No one here would do such a thing, *jefe*, no one."

"If you say so. I'll see you in the morning."

The sky was still gray when King crossed the courtyard to Clint's room. He had slept a little. He didn't stop to knock. He just opened the door and stepped in. He was glad Mercedes wasn't there.

"Clint, roll out of there and get dressed. We've got some riding to do."

Clint sat up in bed. "What's going on?"

"Don't yell now, boy. I've got about the best news you'll ever hear."

"Well, don't just stand there like a stump, tell me."

"I've found Dad's horses. All of them."

"Are you loco? Found the horses. What are you talking about? Alvaraz and his men drove them to Mexico."

"No, he did not. I don't know why, but he drove them southwest to Lost Valley. Remember when I used to hunt over there with Benito years ago? Well, Alvaraz ran them in there and blocked the entrance with wire and cut poles. There's plenty of water and grass for ten times that many. They've probably never even tried to get out. You and Billings never actually tried to track the herd or you'd have surely found them."

Clint put his hand over his mouth. "I can't believe it. Can we get them? Will we have to fight?"

"I don't know about that. Something is going to pop soon. There's something else that happened that you don't know about."

"What now?" Clint was pulling on his boots as he looked at King.

"I killed Hank Billings yesterday morning up at the cabin."

"Killed him? What happened?"

"I invited him to draw. He was slow. Mercedes was there when it happened. I figure that's the reason she isn't here."

"I can hardly believe it, King. All this will turn that murdering Alvaraz loose. Mercedes will tell him about Billings and he'll ride in here shooting."

"We may be ready for him by the time he does. I've sent for Luke Wilson and the Quivira bunch. They'll be here in four or five days. Alvaraz doesn't know how much I know about him. He'll go slow. If he attacks us, he'll have to kill us all and he knows that. I don't guess it would bother him any to kill Mother and Sue Ellen, but he might think a little bit about having to kill all the Mexicans down in the village. It would be hard for him to be sure he got everyone and he couldn't afford to leave a witness."

"Let's get moving. If anybody saw my tracks at Lost Valley, we may have to drive those horses past Alvaraz and his men to get them home. I don't think we'll have any trouble, though. I followed the tracks of a group of riders to the valley entrance. From the looks of the trail, they checked on the horses and left. They probably won't see the need of coming back for a few days."

"King, this is mighty risky," Clint said. "Alvaraz wants this ranch more than he wants anything else in this life. He raves about it—swears it belonged to his family. He'll do anything to get it back."

"What does he plan to do, retire from robbing and killing and become a gentleman rancher?" King sounded disgusted. "Come on."

They found Juan and Eduardo and five other *vaqueros* mounted and waiting. Neale and Daniel Hastings stood beside their horses, talking to Willis.

"I packed some grub," Neale said.

"Good," King said. Taking Ranger's reins from Juan, he swung up into the saddle.

"Stay close to me. We'll stop at the river and work our

way up to the valley. Be as quiet as you can. We'll go in on foot and if there's any of Alvaraz's men guarding the entrance, we'll just start shooting.

"We'll have to clear the fence. It's mostly dead cedars; we can pull them out of the way with ropes. A couple of men can stay outside the valley to haze the horses down toward the river when we get them out.

"Willis, here's the key to the gun cabinet in Dad's office. Get the Sharps rifles and climb up on the roof. There's plenty of ammunition in the cabinet. It's my guess that nothing will happen, at least for a few more days, but I want to be ready if it does. It would take an army to get past you on that roof with a good gun. The Sharpes gives you enough range to pick off a rider before he can get anywhere near enough to do any damage. Jeff will ride in here with Luke Wilson and some other men about Saturday morning. Don't go shooting them by mistake."

Willis reached up to take the key and saluted King without speaking. He turned toward the house, motioning for his brothers to follow.

King felt safe with Willis Hastings in charge. Although he was the silent one of the Hastings brothers, King knew he did whatever was put before him with a determination that allowed no room for failure. Alvaraz would pay dearly before he reached the walls of Blanco Sol with that man up on the roof.

"Let's ride, boys," King yelled, putting spurs to Ranger.

The men held their horses to steady canter. The next twenty-four hours would tax men and horses to their limits. Even if Alvaraz kept no lookout posted in the valley, clearing away the dead cedars and the wire and driving more than a hundred horses back home would be enough.

Clint held his mount close beside Ranger. He seemed to have grown in stature since King told him he found the horses. His face was set and determined.

The sun was well up when the riders crossed the river. They pulled up on the south side and bunched around King.

"Loosen your pistols and carry your carbines in your

hand," King instructed. "Clint and I will go in first. Eduardo and Juan, you hold our mounts at the bottom of the hill, below the entrance there. When we clear out any skunks that might be hiding in the valley, I'll send back for some of the saddled horses. You and Juan stay outside here so you can turn the horses toward the river when we bring them out."

The men walked their horses up the approach to the valley. No one spoke as they dismounted and handed their reins to Juan and Eduardo. King led the way toward the entrance with his gun ready, keeping close to the wall as he had the day before.

They heard no sound from beyond the cedar fence. As it came into view, the men slowed down and crept along with their guns ready. If any lookout were posted, they knew he'd be just beyond the fence.

King stopped at the barrier. Motioning for Clint to stay where he was, he dashed across the open space and knelt beside the wire. Reaching into his pocket, he produced a pair of wire cutters. At his signal Clint came forward and started cutting each strand at his end as King cut his. They cut the top strand at the same moment. The makeshift gate flopped down to the ground. If anyone were in the valley, that sound would surely start them shooting.

The crash of the gate reverberated off the valley walls, and then there was complete silence. They were both ready, guns held for action, but there were no guards. King pushed carefully around the pile of cedars, keeping his head low. A few of the horses were close to the opening, standing with their heads high and their ears erect in alarm. When King suddenly came into view they pounded off.

"Think you're wild again, huh? I've got news." He chuckled. "You'll soon be carrying saddles again. Drovers, too."

Clint look disappointed as he sheathed his gun. "Heck, I was all set to cut loose when that gate came down."

"Don't let it worry you. We'll be tired of shooting before this thing is over." King grabbed one of the poles tied to the wire and started pulling it into the rocks. "It's plain unbelievable how arrogant some people can be," he said. "That

Spaniard never thought of anyone finding this place. He never even set a guard. Just sent some men by here to check every once in a while." He turned to Clint. "Go call the men. Tell them to bring their horses."

It took an hour of hard, dirty work to clear the trail of the dead cedars and wire. The dry, hard limbs stuck up like spears, ready to rip open the belly of a running horse. Every piece had to be cleared out of the way.

The men gathered around to eat their cold meal before they started to round up the horses. King watched Clint as he rested his head against a tree. He had worked harder than the rest of the men. Sweat ran down his face. He looked younger and happier than he had since King had come home. He removed his hat and wiped his face with his sleeve. His brown hair was damp and wavy. The recovery of the herd would lift the terrible burden of guilt from his shoulders. He either hadn't thought about it or didn't care what Alvaraz might do when he found out.

"Let's bunch those horses and get moving, Clint," King said, reaching over to give his brother's shoulder a push. "I want Dad to look out of his window in the morning and see them grazing down by the creek."

"It's like a miracle, King. I just can't take it in. Dad will get well all in a day."

"Don't be expecting too much, now. He's better already, but it'll still take some time for him to get his strength back."

"I know that, but I think he was sicker over me than anything. This will make him willing to at least look at me again, I hope."

"Dad will forgive you, Clint. I know he will. Things are starting to come our way."

The men rode around the bunched groups of quietly grazing horses. The valley swept down in a huge bowl shape, then rose sharply to a forest of pine and cedars. There were five springs in a group watering the heavy grass. The main herd stood near the springs, in among the trees. The riders separated and worked their way through the trees until they were above the horses.

King could hear an occasional yell from left or right of him as the men gathered the horses. The Durango whites moved along quietly. They acted almost as if they were glad to see men again. They swept the other horses along with them. He saw some yearlings here and there, last spring's foals.

The final count will be well over a hundred, King thought. *If we can get this herd back and keep them. A ranch with almost two hundred horses like these won't be poor any longer, I can convince Dad to cut out a bunch to sell—at least enough to finance the cattle drive.*

Ranger was hard to hold as he got near the white stallions. They would occasionally blast a challenge to him and he would trumpet back defiantly. King held him with an iron hand. The horse wanted to fight.

"Behave yourself, you wild man," he said, pulling him down. "You fellas can settle your differences later." The big horse calmed a little at the sound of his voice.

The horses didn't want to leave the valley, but the gathering herd pushed the leaders up to the narrow trail. Slowly they filed out, two or three abreast. Their hooves pounded against stone, filling the valley with sound. Dust rose in a cloud over their heads. The riders covered their faces with their neck scarves. It took most of the day of hard, punishing riding to get the last of the horses through the narrow passage.

At last the riders were back together. Riding behind the last of the horses as they approached the opening, King yelled, "Hold up a minute, fellas."

"What say, boss?" Daniel Hastings yelled back. "I can't hear a doggone thing. My ears feel like they're plugged. That racket musta busted my eardrums."

"You'll live," King said, laughing. Daniel and the other riders were covered in the fine dust kicked up by the horses' hooves. Their faces and clothes were gray and their horses were smeared with dust and sweat. They stopped near the valley opening and slapped their chests and shoulders to knock some of the dust off.

"Get your guns ready, boys. I'm going to yell to the *vaqueros*. If they don't answer, we may have to ride out shooting." Turning away, King guided Ranger almost to the opening.

"Hey, Juan," he yelled, cupping his hands around his mouth. The answering shout was welcome. The men were tired and they were in a tough place. If they had to fight their way out of the narrow opening it would take time and someone was sure to get hurt or killed.

King edged Ranger around the brush and out into the open. He could see Juan and Eduardo at their posts. He answered their wave with his own. The horses were bunched beautifully, drifting almost to the river crossing. "Look down there," he said as the riders joined him. "This is going to be a Sunday school picnic, all the way back to the ranch."

"Yippee," yelled Clint. He spurred his horse around King and clattered down the trail.

"Keep them bunched like they are, men. We'll push them along easy and hold them in that big flat between the village and the creek. We'll reach the ranch house by daylight tomorrow."

The horses gave them little trouble. The big white horses scented home and moved along in a body, sometimes breaking into a trot. The sun was shining when they reached the ranch. The Durango whites picked up speed and soon the whole herd was running. The riders had to whip their tired horses to head them and push them down the slope toward the creek.

When the herd reached Willow Springs, they turned south and flowed out over the flat pasture in grass that reached their flanks. The horses began to mill around and finally settled down to graze.

Juan rode back to King. He was a superb horseman. He moved with his horse and pulled the gelding to his hind feet with a flourish as he stopped.

"I will get some of the young boys at the village to watch the herd today, *jefe*. Eduardo and I will rest and be ready to guard them tonight. They are content to reach their home and will give no trouble."

"Thanks, Juan. I'll not worry about them. You keep them well guarded. Hire what men and boys you need to watch and let me know. I'll pay them."

"*Si, jefe*. The horses will not be taken again."

The men were exhausted. They rode into the corral, pulled off their saddles and bridles and turned their horses loose, then headed straight for the bunkhouse.

"Everything looks quiet at the house, Clint," King said. "I saw Ben up on the roof waving at us as we rode in."

"Thank Heaven for that. I was afraid Alvaraz and his gang would come looking for me before we got back."

"I don't really expect that Spaniard to face a real fight. He likes better odds then he can get here. He'll try some trick first. We can bet on that."

"Hey, boys," Ben yelled from the roof of the house. "That was quite a show. Them horses was a picture pouring across the hill. Ain't nobody going to sneak up on us, boss. You just relax." Waving his hand, the boy returned to his position on the roof.

When Clint and King entered the dining room, Katherine and Sue Ellen were serving breakfast. "I'm sure you're starved, children," Katherine said calmly. "Sit down and eat. You can clean up later."

"Aw, Ma," said Clint. "We're pigs. Put our plates outside."

"I will not," Katherine said sharply. "Sit down and eat your breakfast."

King went over and kissed his mother without touching her with his hands. "I guess I'm surely a pig, Mother, but I sure am glad to mind you right now. We'll be grateful to eat."

Sue Ellen went in and out of the room several times while they were eating. She smiled when she met King's eyes.

"Can I trouble you to pour me another cup of coffee, Sue Ellen?" he asked her.

She stood close beside him to fill his cup, closer than necessary. After a moment she retreated to the kitchen.

Katherine watched them eat. When they finished she said, "You two must be full enough to talk now. I saw you bring in the horses. Your father is standing at his window. He saw you as well. He's been watching since yesterday morning when Neale Hastings told us where you were going."

"How did he take it, Mother?" King asked. "Is he all right?"

"I think he's amazing. He's been much better since you brought Renato into the courtyard the other day. It's like a miracle how much strength he has."

"Did he mention me, Mother?" Clint's eyes showed his fear and hurt over the break with his father.

"Clint, when he saw the horses come around the village, the first thing he said was, 'Clint is with them.' I think that meant a lot to him for some reason. Your father believed you were drinking too much and he was very disappointed in you."

Clint burst into tears. He jumped up from the table and ran out of the room.

"Mother, Clint's all right now. I sent Mercedes home to her father. She was a lot of his problem."

"I wondered where she could be. Sue Ellen and I realized she wasn't in her room yesterday. I must admit it made me nervous."

"I don't think you need to worry. This house is a fort. I'm going to have some of the men cover the windows and do some other work to make it safer. I've sent for Luke Wilson and some more men to help us. Alvaraz will need to lead an army to get to us here."

"You don't think he would really attack us, do you?"

"Not really. It's not his style. He likes to strike in the dark when everything is in his favor. He knows I'm here and I'll be ready for him."

"But why, King? What is he really trying to do?"

"Alvaraz has always wanted Blanco Sol, you know that. He believes our ranch was once part of Riza. I honestly think he's gone a little crazy with wanting it. His ranch doesn't have the water we have, and he's broke, like most ranchers are right now. The last years have been hard on everybody.

"There's thousands of wild Mexican cattle roaming along the brakes of the creeks and rivers and they're going to make us rich in the next few years. Alvaraz can see what's going to happen. I think he figured that with Dad sick and Clint drunk all the time and married to his daughter, he would have a clear field to get the ranch. He didn't count on me coming back to life to interfere with his plans.

"He pushed Clint into marrying Mercedes. He planned on being able to control him through her. Dad's stroke was just good luck for him. I think he was holding that horse herd in Lost Valley until he could get hold of this ranch. He was evidently planning on bringing them back here then."

"What will you do? We can't live as prisoners here in the house, always afraid of what he might be planning," Katherine said.

"I'll find a way—don't you worry about it. You and Sue Ellen just go along as you usually do. We don't want to upset Dad any more than we can help."

"He's come so far in the last two days I can hardly believe it. I think he'll be himself again in no time."

"I can't tell you how happy that makes me. Things will straighten themselves out, you'll see. I've got to get some sleep. It's been a long time since I stopped. Tell Dad I'll see him later." King left the dining room and walked along the porch to his door.

Someone had placed a tub of hot water and a stack of thick towels beside the fireplace and lit a small fire. King peeled off his filthy clothes and slid gratefully into the water. Clean again, he partially dried himself and fell into his bed.

A pounding at the door woke him. He sat up quickly and grabbed a blanket to wrap around his waist. He yanked the door open. Sue Ellen stood on the step. Her eyes swept his bare chest and shoulders.

Blood flew to her face. "Oh," she whispered. "Your mother asked me to wake you. Supper is over. She saved you a plate." She turned her face away as she spoke.

"I'll be right there, Sue Ellen. Thanks."

King grinned at her embarrassment. He could hear her footsteps almost running on the stones as he shut the door. *I'll bet she never saw so much of a man's skin before.* He chuckled as he dressed.

Clint was waiting for him in the dining room. Rosita ran out of the room as King entered. He patted Clint's shoulder and said, "As soon as I eat something, we'll go talk to Dad."

Clint held his head down for a moment. "Do you think he'll talk to me?" His eyes were tormented.

"Of course he'll talk to you. Just let me take the lead. He'll forget he was ever mad at you at all."

Clint watched King quizzically as he ate. When they finished he meekly followed him along to their father's room. As they came in the door, Lambert Sutherland turned and looked at them. His eyes looked alive again. They flashed from King to Clint.

He held his hand out to King. "You found my horses." He clasped King's hand in his, standing up to face him.

"We found the horses, Dad. Clint and I found the herd together."

Sutherland turned to face his younger son. His eyes were confused as they searched Clint's face. "You found them?"

Clint glanced toward King, who smiled and nodded. Dropping his father's hand, King stepped aside as Clint said, "Yes, Dad. We got them all back. There's some white foals with the bunch, too."

Lambert reached out for Clint with both hands, "I've wronged you, son. I thought you and that snake Billings—"

"It's all right now, Dad, forget it," begged Clint. His head was against his father's shoulder. King could see tears in his father's eyes.

King sat down on the bed and watched. Clint looked slight held against his father's tall frame. Lambert Sutherland wasn't really old. He looked more than his fifty-two years still, but years younger than he had only a few days before.

He'd be out and around soon. King wondered if the men would still call him *jefe*. Time would tell. His father wouldn't let him run the ranch six years before, but things were different now. *I'm different now, and so is he,* he thought.

Clint smiled happily as he and King left their father's room. With Hank Billings dead and Mercedes away from the ranch, Lambert Sutherland need never know the extent of Clint's involvement with Alvaraz.

They stopped at King's door. "King, how can I say thank you? Dad believes I was searching for his horses all along. You saved me."

We're not out of the woods yet, brother. When Dad gets out again, he's going to hear things. We've got to do something about Alvaraz. Get your rest, Clint, you're surely going to need it."

King stood in the doorway of his room watching Sue Ellen as she helped Rosita hang clothes up to dry. Her sleeves were rolled to her elbows, showing her round arms. Her dark hair had been done up in one long braid that hung below her waist. It swung gracefully across her shoulders as she bent to pick up the clothes out of the basket and hang them on the line.

Every time I see her I have trouble breathing. Mother is right. She'll make someone a fine wife.

Willis Hastings suddenly appeared at the edge of the roof. "Riders coming, King. Looks like a dozen or more. From the northwest."

"Get down and come to the gate. Tell Ben to fetch the boys from the bunkhouse." King reached the front gate running. He unbarred and opened the small door on the side. A large group of riders were coming fast. He couldn't make out any of them. Luke's red horse wasn't among them. Clint ran up, carrying an extra rifle for King.

"Can you see who it is yet?"

"Not yet, but they're coming at a good clip. Get the boys up on the roof. Tell Rosita to grab a horse and go get the *vaqueros.* We may need them."

The riders were close enough for King to see the silver shining on some of their gear. "It's Alvaraz. Riding in here bold as brass. That's his black horse in front with all that silver shining on his saddle. The rider beside him is a stranger."

There were about fifteen other riders; none of them were Mexicans. As they came closer, King recognized Mercedes as one of the riders behind Alvaraz. *Surely he doesn't mean to fight with his daughter along*, he thought.

King stepped outside the small door to face the riders as they came to a halt in front of the closed gate. He held the loaded Sharps ready.

"Stand easy, Alvaraz. State your business."

"My business is with Clint Sutherland." The man beside Alvaraz edged his horse forward and spoke in a loud voice, "I'm Wayne Felton, sheriff of San Antonio. I'm here to arrest Sutherland for murder."

"Arrest Clint for murder, huh? Whose murder are you talking about?" King asked, incredulous.

"One Hank Billings. Don Alvaraz brought his daughter to me. It seems she saw the killing."

Felton was a large man. He appeared almost square-shaped. His face was red and his eyes were light-colored. He didn't look like a gunfighter, but King knew that most sheriffs in Texas had to be good with a gun.

"I'm King Sutherland, sheriff, and I killed Hank Billings. I don't know what Mercedes told you, but it was a fair fight."

"The lady says different, Sutherland. Your brother's got a bad name in San Antonio. Maybe you just better truck him on out here."

"I'm here, sheriff." Clint stepped out the door to stand beside King. "Felton, my brother is telling you the truth. I didn't shoot Billings. If King shot him, it was a fair fight. I'm wondering what you're doing making this lying sneak's play for him."

King stepped closer to Clint. "We're going back inside now. You'd better get yourself back to San Antonio, Felton, if you mean to keep wearing that badge."

King and Clint moved back toward the door. King held

the Sharps level and ready. He stepped inside first. As Clint turned to enter the door, a shot rang out. King heard the bullet hit Clint with a dull sickening thud. He reached out and yanked his brother through the door. Clint fell inside, leaning heavily against King. As King slammed the heavy door shut and replaced the bar, Clint sagged to the flagstones.

King dropped on his knees beside him. "Clint, boy, let me see." The bullet had entered Clint's shoulder from behind. Whoever shot him had been off to the side and caught him as he turned. A .44 slug had passed all the way through his body, tearing a hole in his upper chest. King pulled off his shirt and bound it tightly over the bloody wound.

Neale came up, panting. "Is he dead?"

"Not far from it, I'm afraid. What's happening out there?'

"We took a couple of shots at them and they took off to the north. A bunch of riders led by a fella on a red horse is coming that way, so Alvaraz turned off toward Riza. They've gone out of sight."

"Get help and move Clint to his room. Tell the women to look after him."

King took the bar off the gate, pulling one side open. He stepped back to watch Luke and Jeff pull their horses to a walk as they reached the entrance. The Quivira boys were right behind them.

"Ride on in, boys. This old fort is back in business. I'm some kinda glad to see you."

"Wasn't that Felton, that new sheriff from Santone, with Alvaraz? I thought I recognized his hoss," Luke asked as he dismounted.

"That was Felton. He rode in with Alvaraz and wanted to arrest Clint for killing Hank Billings. We sent him on his way. Someone in that crowd took a potshot at Clint. Caught him in his shoulder. It looks bad."

"Aw, that's hard. Where's Clint?"

"I had some of the boys carry him inside. We'll go in and check on him in a minute. Let's get everybody settled in first."

King called Jeff and asked him to take the Quivira boys

down to the bunkhouse. "Find them all a place to sleep. I'll send Benito down with supplies later to cook up some food."

When King and Luke entered Clint's room, Katherine and Sue Ellen had cleaned Clint up and bandaged his wound. Rosita was sitting on the floor beside his bed, sobbing.

"How is he?" King whispered to Sue Ellen.

"He's hurt badly. We've stopped the bleeding, but he needs a doctor."

"It would take more than a week to get a doctor here."

"I don't know enough to help him. The bullet passed right through his chest. We've cleaned the wound, but he's lost a lot of blood."

"Stop your worrying, girl," Katherine said. "I've seen worse gunshot wounds. Clint will heal. A doctor couldn't do any more than we have. He's young and strong. He'll be fine."

"Thanks, Mother. You're so sweet and quiet usually, I forget how tough you are." King hugged Katherine.

"What a thing to call your mother, Kingsley Sutherland! Tough indeed." She Ellen was indignant.

"Well, strong then, if that's ladylike enough for you."

"Stop being silly," said Katherine. "Take Sue Ellen outside in the air. This has been hard for her."

Sue Ellen flashed a strange look at Katherine and left the room. King followed her, waving goodbye to the astonished Luke. Sue Ellen walked across the courtyard toward her own room.

"Wait up, Sue Ellen."

She ignored King. He stopped in the middle of the courtyard and watched her back. "Coward," he called out. She entered her room and slammed the door.

King went over to the bench and sat down. Taking tobacco and paper from his pocket, he rolled a cigarette. Luke's spurs jingled as he walked over to lean against the bole of the big cottonwood.

"Gimme the makings, King. Mine are in my pack."

King threw the tobacco pouch and packet of papers to him. "What's happening in San Antonio, Luke?"

"I kept hearing folks talking about getting herds together

to drive north next spring. There'll be a lot of outfits going up that trail by the end of May."

"I plan to be in Abilene by June, Luke. We've got a great outfit and the brakes are full of cattle. We've already started gathering and branding cows. The weather stays open here most winters. It gets cold, but if we can work through most of the winter we can start our drive sometime in March."

"If we can leave that early it would make an easier drive. There'd be plenty of grass along the trail. We might run into some flooding that early, though." Luke rolled a cigarette as he talked and looked thoughtful.

"I think we should take a chance on that. All things considered, the earlier we can leave, the fewer problems we should have. The price of cattle should be higher if we can be one of the first herds of the season to reach Abilene. I've got two big problems now. Alvaraz and finding enough money to finance the drive."

"Shore I'd love to help you with Alvaraz, but I've never had any money to speak of, you know that."

"I'll get the money somehow. Jake Weston, over by the Frio, always wanted some of Dad's white horses. I'm going to talk Dad into selling enough of them to get me to Abilene."

"Jake is one man who could still afford to buy horses. That is, if you can talk your old man around."

"I'll make him understand. He's improving every day now. Did Jeff tell you we found the stolen horses?"

"He shore did. That's about the strangest darn fool thing I ever heard tell of. Why in the world didn't Alvaraz go ahead and drive them across the river into Mexico?"

"That's a real puzzle to me. I'm beginning to think he had plans to get rid of Clint and Dad and take over here until I came back and messed him up. He's as near broke as everybody else around here is except for what he can steal. I guess he thought to get our place because it has more water than his and he knows it's covered in wild cattle."

"That might be it. How come he knew what was going to happen to the cattle market though?"

"It wasn't so hard for anybody to figure out that folks in the east would want beef as soon as the war was over. If the railroad hadn't come to Abilene we'd be driving cattle to Galveston and shipping them to New Orleans. We might even be desperate enough to be driving them all the way to Chicago."

"I never rode on a drive all the way to Chicago, but I've heard about them. I understand that it took a year, and by the time they got the cattle there, they were so thin and pore nobody wanted to buy them. I heard it didn't even pay for the work."

"Well, cows are worth more money now than they were then. If we take enough cattle to Abilene it will sure pay for doing the job."

"Let's get back to the problem with Alvaraz, King. What are you planning to do?"

"Alvaraz won't stop until he's dead, so I've got to kill him. I don't know how yet, but I'm convinced that's the only answer. I'm going to keep guards on the roof and start watching Riza. I'm counting on you to help me."

"What good do you figure watching his ranch is going to do?"

"According to Clint, Alvaraz and his men have been raiding stages and wagon trains for a regular thing. We're going to watch him. When he rides out with his gang, we'll rush back here and get the outfit. We'll catch them with the evidence when they come back to Riza. We could stop them in that deep cut just down from the house."

"Well, that's plumb crazy. You can't even be sure he'll ever rob another stage. He might have sworn off it. Quit all together."

"You know better than that, Luke. Alvaraz will keep on robbing and killing until he's stopped. It'll have to be us or the law or some bunch of cattlemen. We've got to be the ones to get him. I want to catch him with enough evidence to prove that he's the one doing the killing. I've got to prove Clint isn't and never has been involved in that."

King jumped up from the bench and began to pace up and down.

"Calm down now, old son. Maybe we can catch Alvaraz with the goods. We'll try it your way. With Clint laid up, he couldn't very well be out at night riding. That ought to prove something if Alvaraz does pull another job. Let's go on down to the bunkhouse and talk to the outfit, King. They'll want to be hearing Clint's story. They've still got doubts."

"Doubts! Why in the devil did they come then?" King's voice was loud and angry.

"You're as ornery as an old range bull today. Just ride easy. Them boys have a right to make sure Clint's on the level. They know you're straight and they took your word about Clint when Jeff come to Santone after us. They still want to hear you say it."

King walked along beside Luke. His anger cooled at his friend's speech. He knew Luke was right. No westerner would risk being associated with Clint if the stories about his involvement in the robberies kept on making the rounds. The men had shown their faith in King by coming to Blanco Sol. He owed them an explanation.

He spent an hour in the bunkhouse. He told the men most of Clint's story, the parts he believed they needed to know. They had all gambled and drank and they knew the lure of either one was the undoing of many a young drover. First one and then another of the men recalled family members, friends, and acquaintances by name who had fallen under the influence of drink and cards. They agreed that most of those men had died as a result. Usually it was gunplay that killed them.

Bill Ewell summed up their feelings. "Shore Clint was a fool, ain't no doubt about that, but ain't we all? I've done my share of dumb tricks and so have most men. We was just lucky not to get mixed up with a lowdown sneaking skunk like that Alvaraz."

"We'll stick, King," he went on to say. "Me and the boys will ride, shoot, whatever's needful."

"I'm proud and lucky to have you and these men with me, Bill. Your staying here will go a long way toward clearing Clint's name. Folks know you're honest and they'll take your riding for Blanco Sol as evidence that the stories about Clint are lies."

King shook hands with each man. He was shaken by the emotion he felt because of their faith in him. "We'll clear out that bunch of sidewinders, then gather and drive the biggest herd of cows Texas has ever seen. We're going to make history with this drive. You boys work with Jeff and the *vaqueros* for a few days. I've got to ride into San Antonio to get some money together and Luke's going to help me do a special job."

Windy Smith laughed at that. "I know what kind of job that slick gun thrower is good at."

"Aw, Windy," Luke said. "I ain't never throwed my gun unless I had to, and you know it."

"Well, you do a good job of it when you do, man. I'm right glad you're with us. I'd shore hate to have you gunning for me."

Luke stomped out of the bunkhouse. The men laughed at his embarrassment.

"Seriously, boys," King said. "Luke and I are going to get the goods on Alvaraz. I'll be sending for all of you one night soon. When I do, there's surely going to be shooting. So you come ready for it."

"You can count on us, boss." Bill Ewell assured him.

King left the bunkhouse feeling strong and sure. The next few weeks would be risky, but he felt confident that they would win through. He'd talk to his father in the morning and ride to San Antonio to see Jake Weston about the horses.

Chapter Six

The talk with his father was harrowing for King. Lambert Sutherland tried to ignore the necessity of selling some of his horses. When he could no longer present any defense, he turned his head away and pouted like a child.

"I know you can hear me, Dad," King said sternly. "You can understand me too. We're broke. We must have cash to live. Those white horses aren't worth Mother doing without."

"Katherine will never go hungry here on Blanco Sol, boy."

"Maybe not, but she'll soon know how broke we are and what a failure this ranch is." King deliberately made his voice harsh. His father turned back to face him. The hurt in his eyes was terrible to watch.

"You're hard, King, just hard. That's nothing but blackmail, pure and simple." Sutherland was angry, but he was defeated. He would never want Katherine to know he had failed.

"I'll pick out the best yearlings and two-year-olds to keep, Dad. I'll keep old Renato and some mares as well. Luke Wilson will help me, you know he can pick a horse. Jack Weston will buy half of the blacks and bays and as many of the Durango whites as we'll let him have. He'll pay top dollar for them, too."

"I swore I'd never sell to him."

"You're being outright selfish. Jake loves a good horse as
well as you do. All you want is to lord it over him that you
have those great horses and he doesn't."

"Humph. I hope he'll finally be happy. He's certainly
tried long enough to get his hands on them."

King felt happy and yet a little sad that he had finally convinced his father to give in and sell some of the horses. His
father had always been proud that he was the only rancher in
the area with a herd of Durango horses. He had gloried in
being the envy of the other ranchers. King knew, though,
that he would see reason when he got used to the idea. His
father would be just as proud of getting rich again on round-
ing up and selling Mexican cattle. When he and Clint got
back from the drive Lambert would think it had been his
idea all along.

Luke and Juan rode out early the next morning to start the
watch on Riza. Juan knew every foot of the country. He'd
show Luke spots on the ridges where he could look down on
the ranch and watch every movement Alvaraz and his men
made.

King prepared for his trip to San Antonio with a clear
mind. He would make a deal with Weston for the horses and
order supplies. He had decided to visit Judge Ralph
Wilkerson, an old friend of his father, and ask for his help
with Alvaraz. It would be safer to have the backing of the
law in what he planned to do. Judge Wilkerson was respected throughout Texas, and if King could gain his confidence,
he would have a much better chance of stopping Alvaraz and
clearing Clint's name.

King was determined to get an opportunity to speak to
Sue Ellen before he left for San Antonio. He had to tell her
he was falling in love with her. She would probably scorn
everything he said, after the way he'd acted, but he wanted
her to hear him say it just the same.

He stopped at the open door of Clint's room. Rosita was
sitting in a chair beside the bed. Sue Ellen was busy straight-

ening the blankets around Clint's shoulders. She looked up
with hooded eyes as King walked in.

Looking down, she whispered, "Be quiet, he's asleep,"

"How is he?"

"Better, thank goodness. He's awfully weak. He needs to
rest and be quiet to get his strength back."

"You think he's going to make it, then?"

"He will, if he doesn't develop a fever. The wound has
closed. If he keeps still so it doesn't bleed any more and it
doesn't get infected, he'll be all right."

"That's a lot of ifs."

"He'll be all right, King. You've got enough to worry
about without Clint. We'll take good care of him. Let's go
outside. I'll close the door. Rosita will stay with him."

"Has she been there all along?"

"Every minute. She won't leave him even to eat. I've
never seen such devotion. It's a pity Clint couldn't have married her instead of that terrible Mercedes woman."

"I'm betting something will work out. I've been getting an
idea about Clint."

"What do you mean?" Sue Ellen matched her steps to
King's and unconsciously walked along with him toward the
seat under the cottonwood.

"I'm not exactly sure yet myself. Once I get it straight in
my own mind, I'll be able to explain."

"You certainly are being mysterious. I can't understand
you at all, King. You are totally different from the picture I
formed of you, on one hand, and then again, you are exactly the wild boy I expected you to be on the other." She
stopped walking and turned to look up at King.

King motioned for her to sit beside him on the bench. "Sit
here with me, Sue Ellen. I have something important to say
to you."

Sue Ellen seated herself on the bench, but carefully kept
as wide a space as she could between them.

"I need to apologize to you first, Sue Ellen, for the way I
grabbed you. I didn't mean to insult you, I swear I didn't."

Sue Ellen stared at him for a long minute. "What else could you have meant? It was a insult, plain and simple."

"Please believe me, Sue Ellen." King reached for her hand but she snatched it away. "It was wrong of me, but I couldn't help myself. When I looked at you that day I just lost control."

"Do you do that often?" The sarcasm in her voice was thick.

"Doggone it all, Sue Ellen, I've had girlfriends, sure, but I've never been serious about one before in my life."

"Don't be ridiculous. You hardly know me. Besides, if you really cared anything for me you wouldn't have treated me like—like I was easy."

King could hear anger and disgust in her voice. He felt his hopes crumbling. "I can't do any more than apologize and ask you to be my wife." His face was pale and his expression serious. His gray eyes searched hers.

Sue Ellen was obviously startled at King's words. The mask of sophistication slipped from her face and she stared back at him in surprise.

King continued, "I don't expect an answer now. I've got things to do in the coming months that will take all my concentration. I'll not bother you again, Sue Ellen, but when I get back from Abilene next summer, I'll ask you that question again."

King left her then, before she recovered enough to speak. She was still sitting on the bench when he left the courtyard.

San Antonio was just waking up when King rode down the main street. Jake Weston had jumped at the chance to acquire the horses he offered him. King's saddlebags held enough cash money to pay the riders up to date and finance the drive to Abilene. He guided Ranger past a few early risers and tied his reins to the hitch rail in front of the hotel.

King recognized no one in the hotel dining room. He found a table and ordered steak and eggs. When he finished eating he ordered another cup of coffee and relaxed for a few minutes, watching what he could see of the town from the window.

The street began to fill up. From the hotel window, he could see almost to the end. The old mercantile store was busy. Wagons were pulled up to the loading platform; a husky young man was throwing boxes and bags of supplies into them. King continued to watch him work for several minutes, enjoying his coffee. Finally, he paid his bill and stepped out to the porch.

A young boy was leaning against the wall of the hotel. His eager eyes impressed King as he approached. "Can I fetch your horse, mister?" he asked. He looked to be no more than eight or nine years old.

"I'm riding that big black there on the hitch rail. Think you can handle him?"

"I can handle any hoss, mister. I'm ten."

"Well now, I thought you were younger."

The boy looked disgusted. "I just grow slow, mister. Are you riding out?"

"Nope, son. I'm looking for Judge Wilkerson's house. Can you tell me how to find it?"

The boy seemed to literally puff up. "I should smile," he drawled, hooking his thumbs in his rope belt and leaning back on his heels like an old man. "I can take you there."

"That won't be necessary." King struggled to hide a smile. "I know the town well, I just need to know where he lives."

"It's on Simmons Street. It's the big two-story house with lots of flowers. It's painted white. You can't hardly miss it."

"How about taking my horse to the livery stable for me? Tell Charlie it belongs to King Sutherland. Here, boy." King flipped a coin into the boy's outstretched hand.

"Gee, thanks, mister. I'll take good care of your hoss."

"Get along then," King called to the boy as he strode down the steps and along the sidewalk toward Simmons Street.

He watched people walking shoulder to shoulder along the main street. Wagons and horsemen were crowding their way back and forth through the street. The place is bursting at its seams. *Texas is changing fast,* he thought.

Judge Wilkerson's house was just as the boy described it. The judge himself opened the door to King's knock and greeted him with his hand out. "Come in the house, son. I'm glad to see you. I heard you were back home. I know Lambert and Katherine are happy. Word got around that you had been killed, and your folks had given you up."

The judge's hair was still thick but completely white. He had been extra tall once, but his shoulders had stooped and King now looked down into his intelligent eyes. He was shocked to see how old and frail the man looked. "It's grand to see you again, judge. Mother is happy and just as lovely as ever. Dad's much better since I've been home."

"That's wonderful to hear, King. I've had people telling me Lambert was helpless after that stroke of apoplexy." Concern clouded the judge's face.

"He never was as bad as people thought, sir. You know how people can make anything worse by their talk. Dad's almost himself again."

Judge Wilkerson led King through the house to enter his office. "That's the best news I've heard in many a year. What can I do for you, King? I know you didn't just come by to call on an old man."

"I sure would have done that if I had time, judge. I've been running like a branded calf since I got back home."

"Is there a problem of law that I can help you with?" King saw a cloud enter the Judge's eyes again. He felt sure the old man had heard some of the talk about Clint and the robberies.

"I need your help, judge. I believe you're aware of the filthy rumors going around about my brother, Clint."

The judge leaned back in his chair and looked speculatively at King. "I've heard some talk."

"That talk is all lies, Judge. It's Refugio Alvaraz and his gang of lowdown scum who're doing the robbing and killing. Alvaraz meant to implicate Clint to keep attention from him. He got something on Clint. It was a gambling debt that Clint didn't want Mother or Dad to know about, and he used it to keep him quiet. Clint was a fool to get mixed up with Alvaraz, but he's clean. He could never kill innocent people like that."

"I'm thankful to hear you say that, King, and I believe you. People who didn't know your family have accepted the stories, but older westerners know better. The son of Lambert Sutherland might drink and gamble and he might turn out mean, but us old-timers knew he couldn't be that lowdown. Refugio Alvaraz, now, he's another matter."

"I don't have the words to tell you how much better that makes me feel, judge."

King was weak with relief. Judge Wilkerson's reaction to the stories about Clint took away his last doubts of finding a way to clear his brother's name and keep the stories from his mother and father.

King outlined his plan to trap Alvaraz. The judge listened with interest. "You plan to ambush them as they return from a raid?"

"That's my plan, judge. I've already got men watching Riza."

"I think that's risky. You could lose some men. It's not strictly legal either, of course. Maybe I could help you there."

"What can you do?"

"I've already written to the capitol for two marshals. That fool carpetbagger who's sitting in our statehouse went and disbanded the Rangers, so I don't know what caliber of men I'll get, but someone should be here any day now. If we're lucky, they'll actually be former Rangers. If I send them out to Blanco Sol as riders, they could be there when they're needed without tipping their hand."

"They're coming here to help the law find out who's doing the robbing and killing?"

"Yes. Something had to be done. We've managed an army escort for most wagon trains lately, but they're passing through too frequently lately for the army to guard them all. We've never been able to adequately guard the stages.

There've been more than a hundred people killed on that trail in the past year. It was accepted as the work of Indians at first, then the rumors started. Someone told someone else that it was the work of a bunch of drovers, led by your brother Clint.

"The story made the rounds and didn't cause too much interest at first. But then people began to look more carefully at the scene of the robberies. They found more tracks of shod horses and men wearing leather boots, sure signs of white men. That gave more weight to the stories about Clint. Alvaraz undoubtedly counted on the fear and horror created by the killings to make people accept the story without investigating much further.

"There's something else I've been wondering about. It's Alvaraz's motivation for implicating Clint in this mess. Did you know that his mother's people used to own the White Sun Ranch?"

"I've heard some talk that Blanco Sol was once in his family, but I didn't know it was supposed to have belonged to his mother's people. I know he wants our ranch. It was beginning to look like he might get it until I came home. With Dad sick and Clint under his thumb, Alvaraz was getting pretty sure of himself."

"I think Alvaraz is laboring under the delusion that the Sutherland ranch has as shaky a title as many of the other ranches in Texas. If that were the case, taking it over might not have been so terribly hard at that. Our law has been mainly a gun up until now.

"Your father is an astute businessman, King. When he bought the land and that old fort he also went clear to Mexico City and found Carlos Montoya, the man who held the Spanish crown grant. He bought the entire grant from him. He didn't have to do it. Most ranchers will have to fight in court for clear title to their ranches some day soon. Your father's titles are as secure as they can be. He even recorded them in Mexico and at the capitol here in Texas."

"I never knew that. I knew there was a lot of free range, but I though most ranchers had regular deeds to their land."

"No." Judge Wilkerson looked upset by the hypothetical irregularities. "Many of the big ranchers just rode in and took over these old Mexican properties. In some cases they never even paid the Republic for them or filed any kind of legal claim."

"Do you mean that if someone could get rid of a family like ours, they could just take over their property and nothing would be done?"

"Legally, there wouldn't be anything to do. There's little law in a new country, King. Property law is the last thing to be enforced."

"That's why I couldn't figure Alvaraz out. It never occurred to me."

"Refugio Alvaraz knows many titles are shaky, as his is. Riza belonged to a cousin of his. I doubt if he could prove ownership in a court of law."

"That's just about the most amazing thing I ever heard, judge. I'm sure glad Dad tied Blanco Sol up tight."

"You don't have to worry any about that, King. You have enough to do to trap that Alvaraz. I'll send those marshals down to you as soon as they get here."

"Before I leave, judge, can you tell me anything about San Antonio's new sheriff?"

"I appointed him, he was recommended to me by an acquaintance in the capitol. He's only been here for a few weeks. Why do you ask?"

"He rode out to the ranch with Alvaraz and Mercedes and a bunch of strangers trying to arrest Clint for murdering Hank Billings."

"Who brought the charges?"

"Mercedes did. She was a witness to Billing's death and accused Clint."

"Stupid. A woman like that wouldn't be allowed to testify against Clint in any court in Texas. The sheriff ought to know that."

"We told them I really did the killing in a fair fight and to ride on, but one of them shot Clint in the back as they were leaving. He's in a bad way."

"I'm sorry to hear that, son. My goodness, I certainly hope he gets along all right. You've had enough trouble. I thank you for the warning. I'll keep my eyes on Sheriff Felton."

"Thanks, judge. I've got a few things to do before I leave town. You've been a lot of help. I'll keep in touch." The men shook hands and King left the house to hurry back toward the main street.

King stopped by the mercantile and left a list of supplies. He planned to send a wagon for them when he got back to the ranch. He collected Ranger from the livery stable and rode down toward the river. When he left the ranch, Luke Wilson had asked him to look up the Jerdone family and take a letter to Sallie, their daughter.

The flats, as the low ground near the river was called, was dotted with small adobe and wood houses, most of them not much better than shacks. Each house he passed appeared to be inhabited. People sat on the doorsteps in front of their doors. King was surprised to see so many young men lounging around doing nothing.

The Jerdone family lived in the last adobe. The house looked as shabby as all the others, but the yard in front was swept clean. A heavy wagon sat against one side of the house with a canvas over it.

The young man King had noticed loading wagons at the mercantile sat on the doorstep. He rose to his feet as King approached.

"Are you Roy Jerdone?" King asked.

"I am. Who might you be?" The boy looked a little defensive.

"I'm King Sutherland, Luke Wilson's friend."

The boy's face broke into a grin. He wasn't over eighteen, if that, but he was tall and rangy, with bulging muscles in his neck and shoulders. His face was open and attractive. His skin was covered in freckles. He had straight blond hair that hung down his forehead, almost touching his blue eyes. "King Sutherland. Well, I'm glad to meet you. Come on in and meet the folks."

Ducking his head, King followed the boy into the dark room.

"Ma, Pa, come meet Luke's friend King Sutherland."

King was appalled at the sight of the tiny, crowded room. It was clean, but the furniture was makeshift. A bed made out of quilts piled on the floor filled one corner. It hardly left room to walk.

A big man limped into the room and stopped to peer at King. He looked to be in his forties. "This is my pa, Mr. Sutherland," the boy said.

King stepped forward to take Jerdone's extended hand. "Luke Wilson told me about your trouble, Mr. Jerdone, I'm sorry."

"I'm glad to finally meet you, Sutherland. Luke speaks highly of you."

Jerdone ignored King's statement about his trouble. He was a fine-looking man, although his face was weatherbeaten from years of outdoor work. His blue eyes were identical to his son's.

"Come in the kitchen and set." He indicated the doorway to another room. He called out as he led the way into the room. "Sallie, put some coffee on to boil. We've got company. This is my daughter, Mr. Sutherland. My wife's been feeling poorly and she's resting some on the back porch."

Curious, King watched for Sallie as he stepped into the kitchen. She was tiny, not an inch over five feet tall. Her coloring was just like her brother's. She looked like a beautiful china doll. *No wonder Luke's so smitten.* Another thought immediately pushed its way into his mind. *This is no place for such a family to be living.*

The girl's voice suddenly reached him. "I said hello, Mr. Sutherland."

"Oh, please excuse me, Miss Jerdone." King pulled his hat off. "You're so pretty I plumb forgot to talk."

"Now, Mr. Sutherland, Luke warned me about you." Sallie smiled sweetly as she turned to the stove to tend the coffee.

I wish people would just keep their mouths shut about me, King thought grumpily.

He took the seat offered beside Roy Jerdone and turned to him. "Luke said you were working in the stage office or the livery. How did the job work out?"

The boy dropped his head. "Aw, I was working for the stage company. There's so many men in town looking for work they let me go to hire an older man. The only work I can get now is loading a few wagons now and then."

The poverty of this family was obvious to King. This explained it. The father apparently hadn't been able to find work either. Taking Luke's letter from his pocket, King held it out and said, "Mr. Jerdone, I have a letter here for your daughter. It's from Luke. My mother wrote it for him. Is it all right with you for me to give it to her?"

Sallie Jerdone shrieked and ran to grab the letter before her father could even answer.

"There you are, Mr. Sutherland. A man can't have much to say where women are concerned." Jerdone spoke seriously but smiled at his daughter. "I certainly couldn't find any fault with Luke Wilson writing to her though. He struck me as a fine young man."

"You're certainly right about that, sir. There's none better than Luke Wilson." Jerdone's praise of Luke made King like him more.

"I need riders, Mr. Jerdone. Could you bring your family out to my ranch and you and your son work for me?" King almost surprised himself. He knew he had to get Luke's girl out of this hovel and this neighborhood before something happened to her.

"I'm obliged, but I ain't much good on a horse anymore. I stove my leg up a couple of years ago. I'm too slow to handle cattle."

"Can you do any other kind of work?"

"I was a carpenter before I came west and I used to do a little blacksmithing."

"I could sure use you if you'd agree to come. There's room at the ranch house for all of you and three years' worth of carpentering that needs doing. Not to mention how much help you could be shoeing horses. Drovers purely hate that job."

The elder Jerdone looked thoughtfully into his coffee cup. "Are you offering me a job because you're Luke Wilson's friend?"

"Aw, Pa," Roy said. "Don't be like that. I want to go."

"Hush up, boy. Let Mr. Sutherland talk." Jerdone watched King's face.

King knew the fierce pride of the small rancher. He also knew he would never fool this man. He looked into Jerdone's eyes and said, "It's partly because of Luke Wilson, I'll have to admit that. He's never had a girl before, Mr. Jerdone. That means to me that Sallie is mighty special. I figure her family has to be special too. It is the truth, however, that I do need a carpenter and blacksmith on the ranch."

Jerdone dropped his head and struggled with what he was thinking and feeling for a moment. When he finally raised his head, he looked over at Sallie. She was holding Luke's letter against her chest and her eyes were pleading.

"I reckon I can't do nothing but accept, Mr. Sutherland, and I'm grateful."

Roy jumped up and grabbed Sallie, swinging her around. "Whoopee, Sis! We're going to get out of this rotten place."

"You kids calm yourselves down," Jerdone thundered. "You'll scare your mother half to death yelling like that."

"When can you leave, Mr. Jerdone?"

"Why, it wouldn't take us no time at all to be ready. We lost everything we had when our house burned. That wagon out there is about it."

"Do you have a team?"

"We had to sell it last month. Money's been scarce since none of us could find work."

King counted out money and placed it on the table. "I believe this will be enough. I need some mules at the ranch. Please buy a good strong pair and use them to pull your wagon out. I'll have to send a wagon in for supplies as soon as I get back home. I'll have the driver come out here and get you. It'll be a little more than a week." King held out his hand to Jerdone as he stood up to leave. The older man shook his hand and walked outside with him. He stood in the yard watching as King rode away.

It was late in the day when King left San Antonio. He considered spending the night in the hotel, but decided he'd rather spend two nights out on the trail. He had the hotel dining room pack up some food to carry in his saddlebags and turned Ranger south.

The weather had started to change. It wasn't really cold yet, but the air felt damp and chilly. King felt sure it would probably storm before he could get home. The second morning on the trail, he woke to feel rain falling on his face. The sky looked ominous. He quickly rolled his bed and caught Ranger. The horse acted nervous, stamping his feet as King removed his hobbles and snorting at the sound of the wind picking up. The temperature had dropped ten degrees in the last few minutes.

"Take it easy, boy." Speaking aloud to calm the horse, King untied a black slicker from behind his saddle and put it on. "We're going to get wet, old horse, sure as shooting, but we'll be home soon."

He climbed into the saddle and turned Ranger south into the wind. The horse knew he was headed home and moved along at a trot without any urging from his rider. About an hour before they reached the ranch house, the rain began in earnest.

King pulled his hat down and ducked his head into the wind and rain. Ranger slowed to a walk as he fought his way against the wind. The rain fell in torrents. Sheets of water washed over man and horse. The force of the wind and rain coming directly from the Gulf made every step Ranger took require double effort.

The wind ripped across King's face, tearing his breath away. After what seemed an eternity, the white walls of the ranch loomed up in front of him. Flashes of lightning guid-

ed him to the corral. King unsaddled Ranger and turned him
into a stall in the barn. He took time to wipe the horse down
a little with his saddle blanket, then ran to the house.

Ben Hastings opened one side of the gate and held it for
King to run through. "Hurry up, man!" he yelled over the
wind. "We'll drown out here."

King helped the boy push the gate back in place and drop
the bar to hold it. They both turned and ran across the slip-
pery stones of the courtyard to the porch roof and the
kitchen door.

"Son of a gun, what an awful mess," King said, stamping
his soggy boots and shaking water from his clothes. "I'll
need to buy a new hat and another pair of boots after this."

"I'm some kinda glad we're no nearer to the Gulf than we
are," said Ben. "This wild mess looks more like the tail end
of a hurricane than a regular storm. Here, King, sit down
here and I'll help you get them wet boots off your feet."

"Thanks, Ben. I'm about frozen. I wasn't dressed for the
Arctic."

"It'll turn cold for sure after this."

"How'd you know I was out there?" King asked.

"We saw you out the dining room window. I figured from
the way you were hunched over on that horse you'd had
about enough of that weather."

"Well, it was kind of you to go out in it to open the gate.
I sincerely appreciate it. Come on, let's get over here closer
to the fire."

Ben and King huddled around the kitchen stove. King
pulled off his slicker and hat and walked over to toss them
outside the door. He grabbed a towel hanging near the water
bench and dried his head and face, then turned to Elena, who
hovered nearby.

"I'm starved, Elena. Would you consider cooking me up
about three breakfasts?"

"There's some meat and bread on the table in the dining
room, señor. Go on through and I'll bring you some eggs and
fried potatoes." She smiled as she bustled around the kitchen
preparing the food.

Neale Hastings and Sue Ellen were sitting at the end of the table. Neale said, "You made a fast trip, boss. Welcome home."

King nodded without speaking. He felt his face flush. The sight of Neale Hastings sitting close to Sue Ellen shocked him. Jealousy and anger and something a little like fear ran through him. Hastings was a fine-looking man, and he had fought for the South. He was exactly the sort of man Sue Ellen would like.

Shaking a little, King seated himself at his usual place and poured a cup of coffee from the silver pot. Finally he looked up at Neale and asked, "Who's standing guard?" His voice sounded nastier than he meant it.

"Ben and Daniel are keeping watch out of the windows. That's how Ben spotted you riding in. It's a little wet up on the roof."

"Have you heard anything from Luke Wilson?"

"Juan rode in early yesterday for more supplies. They've been camping without a cook fire to keep from being seen by any of the Riza drovers."

"Did he leave a message for me?"

"Yes, he did. I couldn't understand it, though. He said to tell you they were sitting in Yaqui's lap. He told me you would understand."

King laughed and said, "That Juan. When we were youngsters we found a cave the Indians used for ceremonies of some sort. It's way up on the face of a hill overlooking Riza. They've certainly got themselves a bird's eye view from the mouth of that cave. You have to climb down an almost vertical hill on a path not a foot wide to reach it. We named it Yaqui's Lap. I can hear Luke cursing Juan every step of the way down that hill."

"Why are you watching Alvaraz's place, King?"

"I'm sure you've heard the talk, Neale. Alvaraz and his men are robbing stages and wagon trains and killing all the witnesses. They try to make it look as though Indians are responsible. We're going to try to catch him with the goods when he comes back from a raid."

"My life, it's hard to believe that even that Spaniard could be so lowdown."

Sue Ellen interrupted. "You're going to catch him, King? Won't his men start shooting if you try to stop them?"

"I guess they might at that," King replied, turning toward her. His eyes caught hers, and he stared directly into them with an accusing look. Sue Ellen quickly dropped her head and left the table without saying anything more. Neale looked at King questioningly. King ignored him, pretending to give all his attention to the last bit of potatoes on his plate.

Neale shuffled his feet and got up to look out the window at the storm. "How long do you think this will last?"

"Probably until sometime tomorrow morning. The creek and the river will most likely leave their banks tomorrow. These storms happen every year or so. There must be a hurricane out in the Gulf. We're just getting a little piece of it."

"If this mess is just a little piece of it, I'm shore thankful I didn't take up going to sea for a living."

"You're right about that." King put down his fork. "You know, working for Blanco Sol could get dangerous enough before this is over. Will you and your brothers go with us when we brace Alvaraz and his men?"

Neale turned to face King. "We'll fight if we're needed. I didn't think you'd feel the need to ask me that."

"You're right, Neale. I'm sorry. I'm a little on edge this morning."

"I noticed that," Neale said dryly. "I would ask one favor."

"What is that?"

"When the shooting starts, leave Ben out of it."

"You have my word. I'll have an important job here at the house for him to do."

"Thanks. I'll go sit in your dad's office and watch that side of the house. I can't believe anybody is crazy enough to be out in this mess if he can help it, though."

King watched Neale leave the room. It was obvious that Neale understood that King was jealous of his attentions to Sue Ellen. Jealously was a new feeling for King and was an altogether unpleasant one. He threw his napkin in his plate and padded through the hallway to Clint's room. He stopped at the open door. Rosita was sitting in a chair beside the bed. Clint was asleep. He looked pale and still. King leaned one shoulder against the doorjamb and watched Clint and the girl for a moment.

If Clint lives through this, he'd be better off away from here; he thought. *Married to Mercedes, he's bound to be pulled back into something crooked someday. Even if Refugio Alvaraz and his wolfpack are wiped out. If she knows he's still around, Mercedes will eventually come back here and make trouble.*

Rosita would depend on Clint and he would be forced to be a man to take care of her and their baby. King quietly left the doorway and went back to the dining room without disturbing them.

The storm was still raging as King ran from the kitchen door to his own room. He stripped off his wet clothes and dried himself with a towel. Exhausted, he fell into bed and was asleep in seconds. The sun was just rising when he woke up. He looked outside and realized he had slept through the day and night. Dressing quickly, he yanked on a dry pair of boots and ran out into the courtyard. The storm was over.

Limbs and debris from the cottonwood were all over the stones and in the spring. King walked over to the ladder and climbed up to the roof. The land looked as though it had been washed fresh and clean. Turning toward the creek, he could see horses near the bunkhouse. A little farther on were groups of cattle. There were large groups of cattle almost up to the corrals.

King's eyes moved to the south. The creek had left its banks and looked more like a long lake than a creek. The water filled the low thickets of willows and cane and the cattle were forced to higher ground. There were literally hundreds of cattle in sight. King stared transfixed for a moment, then turned and dashed for the ladder. He ran toward the office calling Neale Hastings' name.

Neale burst out the door as King reached it. "What is it? What's happening?" he asked.

"Something so great I'd never believe it if I hadn't seen it with my own eyes." King was grinning from ear to ear. "Get Ben and come up on the roof. You'll never imagine what that storm did for us."

Shaking his head, Neale ran across the courtyard calling Ben. The two men followed King back up the ladder. King stood up on the roof and waved his arms at the groups of cattle. Their black hides glistened in the sun.

"Well, I'll be," Neale said. "Those fool cows are begging to be caught. We could have a round-up if we had a place to hold them over the winter."

"That's just it, Neale. We've got the perfect place. We can drive them east to Indian Creek. There's a big basin where you could hold thousands of cows forever with three or four drovers. It's on a slope, so it won't be covered in water. We can round up right now and brand them through the winter."

"Whoo-wee," yelled Ben, slapping King's shoulder. "That sure is luck, King. Wait until the boys see that."

"It's about time we had some luck, at least some of the good kind. The water is working for us in more ways than one. Nobody can be riding very far in the next few days. There's another big creek between here and Riza that'll be worse than this. Alvaraz can't reach us and neither can Juan and Luke. We'll just get out there and take advantage of this. Let's go tell the outfit."

King and the men spent the next several days driving bunches of cattle east to the Indian Creek basin. The cattle were wild, but they seemed to be frightened and confused after being driven out of their hiding places by the water.

The men gathered every cow possible before they could go back into the cane thickets and get lost again. They rode from dawn to dark every day. By the afternoon of the fifth day, the water was almost down to normal and there were over three thousand head of cattle and a few wild horses trapped in the basin.

King left Eduardo and his *vaqueros* to keep the cattle away from the brakes and rode back to the ranch house with the rest of the Hastings brothers and Jeff. As the tired group came in sight of the house, King saw Sue Ellen waving from the back gate. He spurred his horse forward.

"Luke Wilson is here." Her eyes were full of fear and her voice trembled. "He says to tell you it's time to ride."

"What sorry timing," King blurted out. "There's supposed to be two marshals come from San Antonio to go with us. I hoped this would hold off until they got here."

"I think they're here, King. Two men rode in from San Antonio around noon today. They said Judge Wilkerson sent them to ask you for a job working with the cattle. They didn't look like ordinary riders to me. They're in the bunkhouse."

"Thanks, Sue Ellen. I'll see you later." King turned his horse away and walked him toward the bunkhouse. It seemed as though he could feel Sue Ellen's gaze on his back.

When he reached the hitch rail at the bunkhouse, he turned to see her still standing in the gate, a slim little figure in a light-colored dress. It lifted his heart to see her still there. She was obviously concerned about him. Maybe there was hope for him yet.

When he stepped into the bunkhouse, his eyes immediately went to two men standing against the wall behind the stove. They looked like gunfighters. Their lean, lithe bodies were dressed exactly alike in dark clothing. They both wore their guns low on their right thighs. Their faces had a quiet sternness and their identical blue eyes examined King intently.

"Howdy, marshals, I'm King Sutherland. Welcome to Blanco Sol."

The older of the two men stepped forward and offered his hand. "I'm Jed Race and my partner here is Randy Wingfield. Judge Wilkerson sent us. He explained everything." His voice sounded educated, but soft and drawling, like he might be from east Texas.

King shook Race's hand and nodded to the other man. "I'm pleased to have your help. My man says Alvaraz and his men rode out earlier, so we have to move fast. Our information is that they only ride northwest when they're planning a raid. Get some grub with my men and we'll ride in an hour."

"We'll be ready, Sutherland. Do you have a plan laid out? You know the ground around Alvaraz's place well, I understand."

"Yes, I do. There's a place near the ranch house where we can easily trap him. We may have to clear out a guard or two if he leaves them at the house, but once we're in place and set, he won't be able to get past us."

"We should try to take them without shooting. We have little hard evidence to prove that Alvaraz is the one leading the raids. If we catch them with stolen goods, we're all right, but I'd hate to come out shooting and be in the wrong." Race's eyes bored into King's as he spoke.

King felt cold as he realized these men looked a little wary of him. They made it plain they weren't completely convinced of Clint's innocence. It occurred to him that they might even be a little suspicious of him.

"There'll be proof. I just want you to be there to see it. We won't shoot unless we're forced to it." King's voice was cold.

He turned quickly and left the bunkhouse. The riders crowded around outside the door. "Neale, you boys get yourselves fed and be ready to ride. We may be out two or three nights. Every man pack a rifle and plenty of shells."

"Right, boss, we'll be ready. I'll get you a fresh horse. Old Ranger is pretty worn out right now."

"Thanks. I'll walk back down here after I eat," King called over his shoulder as he headed for the house.

Luke was eating at a table outside the kitchen door. Katherine and Lambert Sutherland were sitting with him.

"Come eat, honey," Katherine said. Her voice was shaky and her eyes looked worried. She filled a plate from the dishes of meat and vegetables on the table and set it at the place beside her. King sat down and began to eat. He would have to explain what he was doing without implicating Clint. He avoided his father's eyes while he collected his thoughts. After a few minutes of undivided attention to his food, he spoke to Luke.

"Judge Wilkerson sent two marshals to trap Alvaraz and his gang. We're going to back them up."

Luke looked at him carefully. He had been uncomfortable sitting there before King joined them. Katherine and Lambert Sutherland had wanted to know why he was watching Alvaraz and his men. He had avoided their questions, waiting for King to explain his actions to his parents.

"The marshals are sure Alvaraz is their man?"

"There's no doubt in Judge Wilkerson's mind. He expects to prove Alvaraz is responsible for all the recent stage and wagon train robberies."

"That lowdown sneak," Lambert Sutherland almost shouted.

Katherine joined his condemnation of their neighbor. "He pretends to be a fine Spanish don. I've always hated him. He never would try to make Riza pay. I certainly never thought he was low enough to rob and kill poor innocent travelers for a living, though."

"That's shore what he's been doing, Mrs. Sutherland," Luke said. "Him and his gang of cutthroats pretend to be a band of Indians. It took a long time for people to catch on, but you can't hide something like that forever. They left shod horse tracks, boot tracks, and other signs that didn't add up for it to be Indians. People talk and now all the talk is about Alvaraz."

Luke looked over at King when he finished.

King stood up. "Ready, Luke? We can't sit here all day. I'll see you at the bunkhouse."

Luke jumped like he'd been shot. "Thanks for feeding me, Mrs. Sutherland. It shore was good."

"You're welcome at my table any time, Luke, you know that." Katherine had always shown a fondness for the shy young cattleman. He and King had been friends since they were boys. He was almost a part of King, in her eyes, and therefore precious to her. Luke nodded to Lambert Sutherland and rushed through the gate and along the path to the bunkhouse.

King stopped near the gate and turned back to the house

to speak to his mother again. "Mother, when Benito and Jeff get back here with the wagons there'll be a family by the name of Jerdone with them. The girl is Luke's sweetheart. I met her when I was in town and she's a dear little thing. The family's had a rough time the last few years. I didn't meet the mother, I understand she's sick, but they're nice folks. There's a boy too. He's going to ride for us. The father is a carpenter and a smith. Please make a place in the house for them. I know you'll make them welcome."

"Luke Wilson's sweetheart! Why, that's wonderful. I know he never had girlfriends like you did. He was always so shy. Maybe he just waited for the right one." Katherine smiled over the idea.

"Now Kate," Lambert said, smiling down at her. "That's just what you need to make you happy. You've always loved a romance."

"There might be more than one romance here, I'm beginning to think." Katherine looked at King questioningly.

King said nothing. He leaned over and kissed his mother's cheek and left them. He could hear her soft laugh as he walked away. She could always tell everything that was going on.

The riders met Juan at the foot of Yaqui Ridge. It was dark. They gathered around Luke as he explained the lay of the land around the Riza ranch house.

"Alvaraz rode out of here with fourteen riders at first light this morning. That leaves two men at the house with Mercedes. I think we should take the house first. If we get down in that cut with rifles behind us we could get ourselves slaughtered."

"You and I can slip in the house, Luke." King said. "I know the layout. It should be simple enough to put them out of the picture without gunplay. You men ride a circle west of the house and corrals and come up behind that hill. By the time you get in position, we should have the house secure. Juan will show you the way."

"Race and Wingfield here will give the orders. If Alvaraz

and his men should show up before we get there, just cover the road and wait for the marshals to tell you when to shoot. If you hear gunfire back at the house, ignore it."

Race looked the group over. There were fifteen men without King and Luke. "I want Alvaraz alive. Is that understood?" The men nodded their agreement.

Bill Ewell patently disliked taking orders from strangers. He turned to King. "You be careful now, boss. Alvaraz ain't going to be taken alive. You should be there with us when the ball opens."

King reached out and placed his hand on Bill's shoulder. "These men will do exactly as I would, Bill. They're here at Judge Wilkerson's orders and on my request. We're safer to have them with us on this."

"If you say so, boss." Bill turned back to Race and spoke with poor grace. "We'll follow your orders, you don't have to worry none about us."

"Thanks," the marshal said tersely. "Let's get moving." He mounted his horse and motioned to Juan to lead the group down the trail. The other men followed silently.

"We can ride as far as that group of cottonwoods," Luke whispered to King, pointing to a dark, wooded area ahead of them. They dismounted at the edge of the trees and led the horses in far enough to hide them. On foot, they left the trees when they got close to the ranch buildings. Now King led the way.

He moved carefully as they entered the corral area, walking beside the stable as quietly as possible. A horse stamped and snorted almost beside them. Motioning for Luke to stay close, King drew his Colt and ran across a small open space to the back of the house. There was a light in the kitchen. King edged his way up to the window and peeped in.

Two men sat at the table playing cards. Both wore pistols. Two rifles lay against the side of the table. King recognized one of the men as Dale Billings, Hank Billings' younger brother. The other was a *vaquero*. His tight black pants and jacket were embroidered in the Spanish style. A huge embroidered sombrero lay on the floor beside his chair. The men's faces were relaxed and their attention was on their game.

King drew back from the window. Keeping close to the wall, he tiptoed to the kitchen door. Luke got in position on the opposite side of the door. King placed his hand on the latch and released it, kicking the door open at the same time.

As he burst into the room, the men grabbed for their rifles. "Hold it, Billings," King said sternly. "Touch that rifle and you're a dead man."

"What the devil are you doing, King Sutherland? Alvaraz will kill you for this," Billings' shouted, his face flushed with anger.

"Drop those gun belts, both of you. I also suggest you be mighty careful how you move your hands." Luke moved around behind the men, a gun in each hand.

King gathered up the guns and moved them out of reach. He tied the men's hands securely as Luke kept his gun on them. "Get in the cellar, Billings. Come on, rider, you too." King motioned to the *vaquero*. The two men stepped into the dark opening and stumbled down the steps.

"It's black as the inside of Hades down here, Sutherland," Billings yelled. "Can't you give us a lamp or a lantern?"

"Get used to it. It's where you belong, Billings." King slammed the stout oak door shut and latched it. He started to prop one of the kitchen chairs under the knob for good measure.

"Don't do that," Luke said. "Let's pull this cabinet in front of the door in case they get themselves loose and try to get out." They pulled and tugged and pushed a heavy oak cupboard in front of the door.

"They'll play hob ever moving that thing even if they do get the ropes off. You stay here, Luke. I'm going to find Mercedes."

"You better be careful. I'd rather go in a hole in the dirt after a rattlesnake."

"She's dangerous, all right. I wouldn't want her behind us with a rifle."

King stepped into the hallway and walked over to the stairs. He knew Mercedes' room was on the north side near the front of the house. Lamps burned low in the upstairs hall. He crept along, checking each closed door as he went. As he opened the third door, Mercedes cried out sleepily, "Who's there?"

King froze for a second, then threw the door open and entered the room. "It's only me, sugar, don't yell," he said reassuringly.

He reached the bed in two steps and sat down beside Mercedes. She had been asleep, propped up on a pile of pillows. Her black hair hung in a tangled riot over her white shoulders. Her eyes were huge with surprise. King reached out and took her hands.

"What are you doing here in my room, King? What is this?"

"I had to see you."

"How did you get past the guards? Papa left Billings and Paco here to protect me." She was getting more and more nervous as she watched his face.

King pulled her toward him as though to embrace her, then quickly snatched a blanket from the bed to pull it over her head. Mercedes burst into frenzied movement. Screaming and cursing, she tried to twist out of his grip. King lifted her in his arms and pushed her into the closet beside her bed. He slammed the door and turned to grab the chair in front of her dressing table to brace under the knob.

"Please, King," Mercedes sobbed and cried through the door. "Please don't leave me here. I'm afraid of the dark. You know that. I'll stifle in here. Please, please let me out." Her voice was soft; she resorted to pleading as she realized she was firmly locked in the closet.

King left the room without answering. He could hear her screams as he ran down the steps and joined Luke in the kitchen.

"What did you do? Tie her up?" Luke's eyes were twinkling. He seemed to be enjoying the sound of Mercedes' screams.

"I locked her in a closet. Let's go." King felt like a heel. That was a lowdown way to treat a woman. He knew it couldn't be helped, though. Mercedes could handle a rifle as well as any man. She could ruin everything if she were free.

King and Luke walked back between the buildings to the stand of cottonwoods. They got their horses and rode boldly across the ranch yard to the front of the house. From there they went straight to the hill where Race and the riders were hiding. Leaving their horses with the others, they ran to join the men hiding among the rocks.

"Everything's secure at the house," King said. "Have you heard anything yet?"

"Nothing yet." Race picked a spot where he could easily step out into the road to confront Alvaraz. "I don't think they'll be here until close to dawn. There'll still be moonlight. We'll keep alert; they have no reason to suspect anything like this. I think they'll just ride right on in. We should be able to hear them coming for a mile."

King took his place beside Race and settled down to rest his back against a rock. He held his rifle between his knees, ready for action. Luke joined Juan and Eduardo at the top of the hill. The *vaqueros* waited to give warning as soon as Alvaraz and his men came into sight.

The waiting seemed to take forever. It was nervewracking. The men didn't speak. They couldn't smoke to pass the time, for fear the smoke would give their position away. The night dragged on. It was almost dawn when the low rumble of hoofbeats alerted them. King looked over at Race. Both men held their rifles ready.

"Wait until they start in the turn and we'll step out into the lane. They'll be walking their horses along here. When I yell, everybody stand up quick and cover a man with your rifle. No shooting unless I start it. That's an order," Race said.

King stepped to the edge of the rock outcropping and waited beside Race. The marshal looked grim. His badge was pinned prominently on his jacket. He looked ready to kill if he had to, but unlike King, he obviously hoped they could take Alvaraz alive. The thunder of the approaching group of horses gave way to the sound of individual horses as the riders moved into the narrow opening between the hills.

Race jumped out almost in front of Alvaraz's mount. "Hold it there," he yelled, covering Alvaraz with his rifle. "You're covered. Tell your men to drop their guns. There's a rifle on every man."

Alvaraz's face contorted in an expression of fury. "What is this? You would hold a man up on his own range, in front of his own home?" He raised his hands high as his eyes burned the marshal's.

"The man said shuck your guns, Alvaraz, and go ahead and drop your saddlebags while you're at it," King said.

Alvaraz turned his head to stare daggers at King without moving. He knew he was caught. The man with the badge would see him and his men hanged when he found what they carried in their saddlebags.

King watched the Spaniard's face. Alvaraz was clearly thinking over his chances. Suddenly he spurred his horse into Race. "Kill them," he screamed to his men, drawing his gun. King got off one shot with his rifle. Alvaraz reeled in the saddle but pulled himself straight and fired. King felt a heavy blow on the top of his right shoulder. He landed flat on his back beside a boulder. His Colt was in his left hand as he scrambled back to his feet.

Race was lying to his right, knocked out when Alvaraz's horse ran over him. King jumped back into the rocks and fired at Alvaraz's back. The Spaniard fell out of his saddle and rolled over. King ran to him and looked down. Alvaraz's eyes were open, his face relaxed.

Shots were booming beyond the turn in the trail. King ran toward the sound. As he turned the corner, the shooting stopped. Three men stood beside their horses. Luke Wilson and Wingfield pointed rifles at them.

"Come over here and tie their hands, Juan," Luke said. "We're going to dump their saddlebags."

A search of the saddlebags revealed all the proof Judge

Wilkerson would ever need: personal items, jewelry, and men's pocketbooks. An unopened bag of mail hung behind one saddle.

Bill Ewell walked around the turn leading Alvaraz's horse. "Take a look here, fellas. That lowdown Alvaraz had a bag of gold tied behind his saddle. I'm guessing he figured the best of the takings belonged to him."

King laughed hollowly. "He got the best in the end. It's a crying shame for him to get off as easily as he did."

"I seen him lying back there, King."

"What are we going to do with his three men, Wingfield?"

"Where's the nearest tree?" asked Bill Ewell.

"There are plenty trees in the yard by the house. Nice big trees," Juan said.

"Luke, you drag them up there and get ready. I'm going to see about Race." Wingfield turned and walked around the rocks.

King was beginning to feel weak now that everything was over. He was steadily losing blood from the wound in his shoulder. "Neale, would you tie a kerchief around my shoulder?" he asked.

"Oh my goodness, boss, why didn't you say something?"

"I just did. Wad my kerchief up against this hole and tie it on with yours. Tie it tight enough to do some good."

Neale rushed to tie up the wound on the top of King's shoulder. The kerchief held the pad against the slice made by the bullet and stopped it from bleeding. King sat still.

"I'll be all right in a minute. It's not much more than a scratch. The bullet went right on through. I just feel weak from shock, I guess."

"Somebody get a blanket," Neale yelled.

"Stop fussing, will you? You're as bad as Mother."

"You need to stop fussing yourself and rest awhile. You'll feel better in a few minutes."

Neale wrapped a blanket around King's shoulders and rolled another so he could use it as a pillow and lean his head against the rock. King closed his eyes and tried to ignore the dull pain that started throbbing through his shoulder.

He woke up to see Luke sitting beside him. "Hey, Luke, what's been happening? Is Race all right?"

"Take it easy, pard. I'll tell you all about it." Luke handed King the cigarette he had just made and started rolling another. "Wingfield and me dragged those three hombres up to the house and put ropes around their neck. You should have seen their faces. We just sort of fumbled around for a while, then took the ropes off. They were so relieved one fella messed his drawers. I think Wingfield felt like paying them back for finding Race lying back yonder with a broken arm.

"The marshals are gonna take them three men into Santone along with all that stuff they had crammed in their saddlebags and let Judge Wilkerson hang them where the whole town can see it."

"Has anybody seen Mercedes?"

"Yeah. Wingfield let Billings and that *vaquero* out of the cellar. They swore they had nothing to do with the robberies and never rode on one, so the marshal told them to get Mercedes out of her room and disappear. The three of them rode off towards Mexico just a few minutes ago. Wingfield looked like he was mad enough to shoot all three of them if they'd blinked at him, but he didn't have no proof on them."

"It's all over, Luke, and Clint's in the clear. I feel like the whole world has been lifted off my shoulders."

"It shore made me about as happy as it's possible to be when Alvaraz busted out like that. He'd have tried to put some of the blame on Clint if we'd taken him alive. I'll bet my horse and saddle on that."

"I know that, Luke. Clint could have denied anything Alvaraz said and he probably would have gotten off in court, but people would always remember. It's much better for him this way."

Bill Ewell drove up in a wagon. Race was resting on a bed of straw and blankets in the back. Luke leaned over King. "Let me help you up in that wagon bed, old son."

King pushed himself erect with his good arm. "I can ride, Luke. Forget it."

"Ride in the wagon, King. It'll be a lot easier for you."

"I'm darned if I will. It's only a little slice across the top of my shoulder. Go get my horse." King stood up. "I'll make it. I'm not going home in the back of a wagon. It would scare Mother half to death."

"I'll ride on ahead and tell her you're not bad hurt. It's a long, rough ride from here back to White Sun."

"Oh, shut up, will you?" King brushed Luke's hand from his arm. "Go get my horse."

The ride home became a nightmare for King. The pain in his shoulder seemed to increase with every step. When his horse reached the bunkhouse, it stopped. Luke was already on foot and ran over to catch King's bridle.

"I'll lead your horse up to the house, King. Get your breath first. You'll scare everybody to death if you go in the house looking like you do right now."

"I'll be better in a minute." King felt exhausted and drained of strength. He sat hunched over in the saddle. His wide shoulders drooped and his head hung down.

After a moment, Luke led the horse slowly to the house and helped King to the ground at the gate. King grabbed Luke's shoulder and hung on.

"I should have listened to you, old hoss. I'm almost too weak to stand up."

"That bandage is soaked. That's what's wrong with you. We'll get it tied up right and you'll be fine in a day or two." Luke held part of King's weight on his shoulder and helped him directly to his own room.

Sue Ellen burst into the room. "What happened—what happened?" Not waiting for an answer, she rushed over to the bed and stared down at the blood-soaked bandage with horror in her eyes.

"It's only a scratch, Sue Ellen. It's nothing to get excited about." King started to sit back up.

"Lie down." Sue Ellen placed one hand on King's chest and pushed him back down against the pillow. Without turning her head, she said, "Go get Katherine, Luke. Tell her to bring her medical box."

"Aw, please don't tell her, Sue Ellen. She'll be upset."

"You men try my patience," Sue Ellen said as she began to unwrap the bloody bandage from his shoulder. "Your mother has seen blood before. She's not going to faint."

Luke left the room. King winced as Sue Ellen pulled the bandage from under his arm. "You don't have to be so rough," he said accusingly.

"I'll get some water and get this bandage off. It looks filthy." Sue Ellen turned to the washstand and picked up the pitcher of water, pouring some into the basin. She dipped a clean towel in the water until it was soaked, then used it to clean the wound.

King's heart pounded at her nearness. Her sleeves were rolled up above her elbows and her smooth arm almost touched his cheek. She carefully looked everywhere but at his face.

"Why don't you look at me?" he asked softly.

She ignored him. About that time, Katherine entered the room with her medical kit. King was feeling so sleepy he hardly noticed the burn of the medicine or the bandage the two women put on his shoulder. He had fallen sound asleep when they finished and left the room.

King felt better when he woke up the next morning. The full night's sleep had made him feel stronger and his shoulder only ached a little when he tried to move it. Katherine demanded that he stay in bed that day. He made a half-hearted attempt to argue, but stayed put and dozed between meals. By the second morning he refused to stay in bed any longer. Katherine made a sling for his arm and it felt comfortable enough for him to get up.

Careful not to jar his shoulder, King walked to the dining room. There was no one around except Rosita.

"Come and sit, Señor King. I will fix your breakfast." Disappearing into the kitchen, she returned in a few minutes with a plate piled with eggs, potatoes, and biscuits and placed it before him. Her head was bowed and she turned her face away as she served him.

"Don't be shy, Rosita." King smiled at the girl. "Come here and tell me how my little brother is doing."

"Clint is healing, señor. He is clear of fever these two days. I am filled with happiness." Her eyes glistened with pleasure as she spoke.

"That certainly is good to hear. Old Clint had me worried there for a few days. Rosita, have you told Clint your news?"

"Oh, señor. I have told him. He wishes to run away from here." A deep red blush burned over her olive skin. It was almost painful for King to see her embarrassment.

"You know something, Rosita? I think that's a mighty fine idea. I was going to suggest to Clint that you do exactly that."

"But there is Mercedes. Clint is her husband. She would not let us go. She would not." Wringing her hands, Rosita was almost crying.

King rose from his chair and patted her shoulder awkwardly. "Hush now, honey. I've got a plan to get you two away from here as soon as Clint's in shape to travel. There's a wagon train leaving Santone in about two weeks. You could ride along with them over to East Bend. Clint and I have an uncle there with a big spread. He could give Clint a job working his horses and would be glad to get him. You and Clint could live there and make a good life."

Rosita's eyes filled with tears. She stared up at King with heartbreaking sadness on her face. "What about Clint's wife?" Despair filled her voice.

King took her shoulders in his hands. "Rosita, listen to me. The devil with Mercedes Alvaraz—forget about her. She's a she-wolf, a lying, sorry excuse for a woman that isn't worth a second thought. Mother and Dad might say Clint made his bed and should lie in it, but I don't feel that way. Mercedes took off for Mexico and might never come back. She knew what her father was doing and went along with it. She probably shared in the profits. People will know that.

"She'll probably never risk coming back to Texas. You and Clint love each other and you have a baby coming. You can't let Clint's stupid mistake in marrying Mercedes for all the wrong reasons ruin three lives."

Rosita began to sob aloud. "Oh, King. It would be so wonderful." She bowed her head against his chest.

King held her in his arms like a child. "Don't cry like that, honey. It'll be all right. I promise you. Let me take care of things. I'll make all the arrangements. Just stop upsetting yourself. It can't be good for the baby."

King heard a slight noise. He lifted his cheek from where it lay against Rosita's black hair and looked up. Sue Ellen stood in the doorway with a stricken look on her face. She stared into King's eyes for an agonizing moment, then turned and ran out.

"Oh, for the love of Heaven. She heard what I just said." King ran his hand over his hair and shook his head.

"Don't worry, Señor King, I will go and explain to Sue Ellen."

"No. I'll go talk to her. You forget about it. She's my problem."

"She loves you, you know."

"I don't know about that, Rosita. She sure has a poor opinion of me if she does."

"I know that she loves you. I have seen her face when she looks at you."

"It's probably disgust you see. She thinks I'm some kind of mad woman chaser or something like that." King's words sounded bitter.

"You are wrong. She would not be so upset by what she heard if she did not care for you."

"I sure hope you're right, little girl. You go on now, I need to figure this out."

Rosita went through the doorway into the kitchen. King rolled a cigarette and paced the floor. He was torn between despair and anger. How could Sue Ellen think what she obviously thought when she saw him comforting Rosita? *I ought to just let her stew. Let her think whatever she pleases. She'll know the truth when Clint and Rosita leave, then she'll feel like a fool*, he thought.

King almost enjoyed the picture he created of Sue Ellen's chagrin. Suddenly he stubbed his cigarette out in his plate and stalked out into the hall. The door to Sue Ellen's room was closed. King stopped for a moment before he knocked. He could hear her crying softly. He pounded on the door with his fist.

"Sue Ellen?"

"Who's there?"

"You know who it is. Open this door. I want to talk to you."

"Go away. I have nothing to say to you. I wish to never see you or speak to you again."

King was trembling with anger. He grabbed the doorknob and turned it. The door gave under his hand. He pushed it open and stepped inside.

"How dare you come into my room? Get out of here this instant. I'll scream this place down."

"You're already doing that." King's voice was cold and harsh. His gray eyes were black with anger. "If you'll shut up your screeching a minute, I'll say what I came to say and get out like you want."

Sue Ellen turned her back to him and went over to stare out the window. The strong sunlight touched her dark hair with red lights. Her pale cheeks were streaked with tears. "Talk then, if you must, and then get out."

"I'll do that." King leaned back against the closed door. "You have a nasty little mind, Sue Ellen, and you're wrong in what you're thinking about me."

Sue Ellen gasped and whirled around to face him. The sad expression on her face hardened to scorn. "I heard you—you and that poor little girl. How could you? How could you be so base?"

"Believe what you like. I've told you. You are wrong—wrong, Sue Ellen. You misinterpreted what I said to Rosita."

"I couldn't have. What you said was plain as day. Rosita is expecting a baby and you stood there holding her in your arms. And you had the nerve to ask me to be your wife." She was so angry she seemed to almost spit out the words.

"I had the nerve because what I'm saying is true. Rosita is nothing to me except a sweet little girl I've cared for like a baby sister."

"I don't believe you!" Sue Ellen fairly screamed the words. She was crying again. Huge tears filled her eyes and ran unchecked down her checks.

King looked steadily into her eyes. He lifted his shoulders from against the door and walked closer to her and almost whispered, "I'm glad you care so much, Sue Ellen."

"No! You devil. No! I do not care. I just hate you! You are a lowdown creature."

"Don't go too far, girl. I'll only take so much, even from you." The expression on King's face was hard to read. He stepped closer to Sue Ellen.

"You've listened to Clint tell blown-up tales about me and then heard Mercedes do the same until you believe every word. You're wrong, Sue Ellen—flat wrong. You're jumping to conclusions again. Rosita is having a baby, that much is right. But she's having Clint's baby, not mine. Believe what you like, but that's the gospel truth."

King turned on his heel and left the room, slamming the door behind him.

Chapter Seven

King rode with the drovers every day, roping and branding cattle. He and Luke gentled young horses and branded some of the older ones. His plan was to fill every day with a frenzy of activities that would keep him away from the ranch house and Sue Ellen while preparing the cattle and outfit for the drive north.

He visited with his brother every evening. Clint was rapidly regaining his strength. His love for Rosita and his delight over their coming child made him impatient to be strong again.

"I feel fine, King," he said one evening as they discussed plans for his trip to their uncle's ranch. "I could leave tomorrow. If we don't go soon we may not be able to get away."

"Don't be so impatient. You know it's a long hard trip. Rosita needs a man to protect her, not a wreck of a man she'll have to look after. You can wait another week. You don't want to have to wait too long for the wagon train after you get to San Antonio."

"Another week—I'll never wait that long!" Clint declared. "I swear, King. I can stand the trip. I've been walking around the courtyard every day and I feel great."

King thought for a moment, then shrugged his shoulders and said, "What the heck. I guess a few more days won't make that much difference. Are you and Rosita packed?"

"We've been ready for days. Rosita is almost crazy with this waiting and so am I."

"Go tomorrow then, Clint. I'll send Jeff and Eduardo with you. As soon as you get to Uncle Merrill's ranch they can come on back here. You and Rosita slip out at dawn. I'll have the boys ready with the wagon. I'll make sure you have plenty of supplies and enough money for you to manage until you get settled.

"You can write Mother and Dad when you get there. They won't like it much, but they'll understand. It isn't like Uncle Merrill ever saw Mercedes. All he knows is that you're married. He needn't know anything about your private life. Rosita will get used to the idea and she'll be happy there."

"I hope you're right about that," said Clint. "That girl is mighty upset over doing things this way, but I reckon she knows it can't be helped."

"Don't even think about it anymore, Clint. A man has to live his life. You know you can't stay here. There'll be whisperings about your involvement with Alvaraz for years. You can't let one dumb mistake ruin everything for you and Rosita. Go on out there and live like everything's right and it will be."

"I'll make things right. Rosita is all I ever really wanted anyway. I'll never know how a grown man could be as stupid as I've been. I owe you my life, King. I'll make what you've done for me worthwhile, I promise you that."

"You don't owe me a thing, Clint. You and Rosita be happy. That's all I want." King clasped his brother's hand. He felt good about Clint now. All the trouble had strengthened him. He seemed older and more serious. He'd be a man to make his family proud.

"Get some sleep, Clint. I'll have Jeff make you a soft bed in the wagon so you can rest a lot on the trail. You'll have to take it slow and let the men do the camp work, but you'll make out fine."

"Good night, King. Thanks again."

King stood at the back gate and watched the wagon disappear into the semi-darkness. He held Clint and Rosita's letters to their parents. He knew there'd be a wild, upsetting time when they read them. They would all get over it, though. Clint and Rosita would make a decent, happy life. That was the important thing.

King finally returned to the house, slipping the letters into his jacket pocket. He planned to hold onto them as long as possible, at least for a few hours. No need to start anything until he had to.

As he walked slowly past the spring, Sue Ellen was suddenly beside him.

"King," she said, laying one hand on his arm to stop him. "Can you forgive me?" Her voice was so soft the words were barely audible.

King turned to face her. Her eyes were pleading. She stood close to him, their bodies almost touching.

"Please say something. I was such a fool. I think I knew it all along." She dropped her head.

King could smell the faint sweetness of her hair. Her forehead touched his chest. He folded her close in his arms. "Hush, Sue Ellen, just forget it." His voice was husky.

"I was so horrible to you," she almost cried against his shoulder.

"Look at me, Sue Ellen." King raised one hand to her chin and pushed her head up so he could see her face. Her eyes were closed. Her lips trembled slightly. King touched his lips to hers.

Sue Ellen opened her eyes. She slid her hands up to King's shoulders and settled closer in his arms. "I love you," she whispered, her lips almost touching his. King kissed her again and again.

"I love you too, sweetheart," he whispered against her mouth. He finally released her and stepped back. He looked down into her eyes, both hands around her waist.

"You did say you loved me, didn't you?"

Sue Ellen smiled. "Yes, I did. I love you. I love you. I love you."

King pulled her to him again and held her close. His head rested against hers. "When will you marry me?"

"Whenever you say."

"Boy, that's a temptation. I'd like to say tomorrow. We'd better make it in late summer, though. As soon as I get back from Abilene."

"Summer is lovely here. Summer will actually be perfect, darling." Sue Ellen smiled up into his eyes. "King, let's go tell Katherine."

"I've got a feeling she already knows, but we can go tell her when. That'll make her happy. Come on."

Grasping Sue Ellen's hand, he led her to Katherine's door. King knocked and called out, "Open up, Mother. I've got something to tell you."

Katherine opened the door immediately. She looked surprised and then smiled with delight as she saw the expression on their faces. "Oh, children, I'm so happy for you. Come in, come in. Sit down. I knew you'd work things out. I could feel the strain you were both under. Sue Ellen, dear, I couldn't have chosen better for my son. I've had hopes ever since he came home."

"Mother always knows everything, Sue Ellen," King said. He hugged Katherine. "You two plan the wedding. I've got work to do."

"Wait a minute before you leave, King," Katherine said.

King turned and looked at his mother. Her tone of voice was suddenly completely different and she was looking at him with a serious expression.

"I hope Clint and Rosita were kind enough to leave a note for Rosita's parents. You know they will be devastated to think their daughter would run off with a married man."

Astonished, King could only stare. He couldn't think of anything to say.

"Did you think I wouldn't know what was going on? That I couldn't see Rosita's condition?" Katherine asked with a smile.

King finally found his voice. "I should have known you wouldn't miss a thing. Clint and I thought we were sparing you, Mother. We did the only thing we could see to do. He loves Rosita, and Mercedes will never come back here.

She's as gone as if she had been killed along with her father."

"I agree with you, son. I do wish you and Clint had trusted me to understand. I would have liked to let him and Rosita know how I felt before they left. I would have given them my blessing if you had seen fit to include me."

"Please forgive me. I only did what I thought was the best."

"You know I forgive you. I just didn't want you to think you had gotten away with anything. Give me the letter and I'll talk to Elena and her husband. I don't think they'll be too upset."

Relieved, King turned both letters over to his mother and gratefully left the room.

The next weeks were happy ones for King and Sue Ellen. They rode together when weather permitted and spent evenings talking in front of the fire. Luke and Sallie Jerdone rode with them occasionally, but both couples slipped off by themselves as often as they could get away.

Both men spent some hours every day helping the drovers with the branding and other jobs needed to get the herd ready. It was much easier with the cattle forced out in the open by the water. The crew could handle many times the normal number of cows a day, since they didn't have to drive each one out of hiding. King picked out young breeding stock to keep and helped the men block off the entrance to a small dell near the ranch house to keep them separated from the herd. He planned to buy a good bull when he got back home and raise a better grade of cattle.

When March came around, the herd was ready. More than twenty-three hundred head of fat beef were branded and ready to drive. With Luke's help, King had chosen a hundred and twenty horses to form a remuda for the drive. Each rider would require remounts constantly on the trail. A good horse could work cattle from dawn to dark, but he needed to rest a day or two before he was ready to work another day.

The horses they chose were all blacks or bays. The Durango whites were strong and were good workers, but were too spirited for trail work. Their shining white coats could also reflect light and might spook the herd some moonlit night.

Ranger learned to work cattle easily. He was intelligent, quick-moving, and wanted to please. He was bigger than most of the other horses. There was hunter blood somewhere in his family background that gave him longer lines and a good four inches in height over the western horses. His speed and stamina would allow him to carry King day after day on the trail. King had grown attached to the big horse and Ranger followed him around like a dog.

Luke spent most of his days working with the horse herd. His ability as a trainer was much more than knowledge. He talked to the horses constantly, calling each by name. They responded to his voice as though they could understand his words. He was unfailingly gentle and kind to them and they responded as if they loved him.

Katherine was planning a double wedding for King and Sue Ellen and Luke and Sallie, to be held as soon as they returned from the cattle drive. She and Rebecca Jerdone spent their days happily sewing and gossiping.

Sallie and Sue Ellen helped make dresses and embroider linens. The women opened unused rooms in the ranch house to prepare apartments for both couples. They kept Sallie's father busy tearing out walls and refurbishing rooms.

King hired two more riders and a cook for the drive, who had stopped at the ranch one day asking for work. Luke knew them and recommended them to King. "I rode with these fellas over to the German settlement. Jim and Billy here stood for that old man Steinbruner's ways longer than I could have, but I know they're good cowpunchers."

"We heard you was going to take three thousand cows up that trail laid out by old Jess Chisum, Mr. Sutherland," said Billy. He was a Texan, built long and slim, and stood almost as tall as King. His pale blue eyes and almost white-blond hair were typical of men from north of San Antonio. "Me and Jim here figured the best way to see a big herd took up that trail was to sign on with White Sun."

"Well, to tell the truth, boys, I'm not taking but about twenty-two or twenty-three hundred head, maybe a little more, but I'm glad to have you with me. Luke says you can both handle cattle and I need every man I can get."

King turned to the grizzled little man beside the cowpunchers. "Luke tells me you can cook."

The man spat tobacco and wiped his beard with the back of his hand before answering. He wore a bright plaid jacket and miner's boots that looked about two sizes too big for his feet. His voice was thin and had a Kentucky twang.

"I kin cook if I have decent gear. I fed Chisum's bunch when they went up the trail. I tried to feed old man Steinbruner's bunch for near five year. That sorry excuse for a somebody was so tight I had to make do for everything I needed. I made up my mind I ain't working like that no more." He stuck his hands in the pockets of his jacket and stared at King as though he dared him to offer to hire him.

"What's your name?"

"I go by Cook."

"Just Cook?"

"If that ain't enough, I can ride my mule out of here just as fast as I rode in."

"Hey, come off it, friend. I'm not questioning you about your name. Cook it will be. I've got a fine wagon and you can pick out your own gear and whatever supplies you need when we hit San Antonio."

The man's expression didn't change. He still sounded angry. "That suits me."

King almost laughed out loud at the man's attitude. He was as testy as a cow with a new calf. "You men can go check in at the bunkhouse. Luke will show you around and help you get settled."

The addition of Jim and Billy gave King twenty drovers, counting the *vaqueros*. He knew they'd all have to work hard, but they'd be able to handle the herd.

The weather improved every day. Luke and King kept busy from morning to night. They would take two wagons, one for supplies and the other for a chuckwagon. Jake

Jerdone examined and tightened and reinforced where necessary, making sure every piece of iron on the wagons was
safe, then put new shoes on dozens of horses.

Jerdone seemed to be twenty years younger since they'd
arrived at the ranch. He looked as though being able to work
and provide for his family gave him a new lease on life. His
work turned out to be invaluable to King in getting the gear
ready for the drive. He, Benito, and Jeff would stay at the
ranch during the drive. With some help from the Mexican
boys at the village, they would care for the ranch and the
white horses. King was thankful for Jake Jerdone's presence.
He would protect the ranch as though it were his own.

One day the weather changed. It was suddenly spring.
King and Luke agreed it was time to start the drive. They
were as prepared as they would ever be. "It's time, King,"
Luke said. "We should start tomorrow."

"There's nothing I can think of to stop us."

"How about I can't even stand to think of being away from
Sallie for near three months. That could almost stop me."

"I know exactly how you feel. We might have left a week
ago. I just couldn't face it then, but I guess it can't be helped.
It's time to go."

"Come on, King, let's go tell the outfit."

Ewell and the riders left the bunkhouse at dawn the next
day to start moving the herd north. It would take all day to
get them from Indian Creek out to the open range. Once
started, the herd would move about ten or twelve miles a
day under normal conditions. But first the cows and riders
had to learn a routine. The men milled about, yelling to the
cattle and swinging their riatas, urging them into a compact
group.

The whole family came outside to watch the spectacle of
the huge herd moving reluctantly out of the lush grass in
the valley up onto the open range. Here and there a small
group of cows would break away from the edge of the herd
and try to make a run for freedom. A rider would dash
toward them, head the group, and drive them back into the
herd.

The *vaqueros* were a joy to watch. Their horsemanship was far above even the Quivira riders', who had been raised on horseback. Their embroidered jackets and trousers and their huge sombreros were eye-catching. Touches of silver decorated their saddles, bridles, and chaps. Their horses had been chosen from the same group as those of the other drovers, but they seemed more fiery and spirited.

The herd moved slowly. It seemed to flow across the range, a great blot of black and brown with touches of white and red that blanketed the slopes.

King stood in the open gate to the courtyard, watching his dream move before his eyes. The herd would save Blanco Sol. Money for living and building was right there in front of him, if he could get the herd to Abilene. They would be on the trail for around three months. The dangers were great to men, cattle, and horses. Some of the stock wouldn't make it. Some of the men might not.

The responsibility weighed heavily on King's shoulders as he thought of Luke Wilson, Neale Hastings and his brothers, and the Jerdone boy. Suppose something happened to one of them or to any one of the riders?

They were all good men, tough and hardened by the winter's work getting the herd ready. He knew they would make it to Abilene if any riders could. Cattle herds had made it up Chisum's trail the year before and many others would follow this year. Maybe his luck would hold.

"Why are you so quiet, darling?" Sue Ellen said. She was standing at his elbow, smiling up at him.

"I was just thinking, honey. Let's go back up to the house." King slipped his arm around Sue Ellen's shoulders and they walked slowly toward the house.

They had said their goodbyes the night before. Sue Ellen hadn't cried, but it had been hard for her to face being separated from King for three months or more. She had held King close, wrapping her arms around him tightly as though she would keep him there by force.

King had laid his cheek against the top of her head. "I'm going to miss you," he whispered.

"Oh King, I'm sick over thinking about tomorrow," Sue Ellen said with a quaver in her voice.

"I have to go. There's no need to fight against it. It's sure gonna be lonesome. I've gotten used to having you close."

"Stop it, darling. I'm almost crying now."

"Kiss me goodbye now, Sue Ellen, and promise me you won't cry when we leave tomorrow."

"I won't cry. I know you'll be fine."

"You bet I will, honey. I'll bring Reverend Dodson with me from San Antonio when I come home. We'll get married the day I get back here."

"I'll be ready and waiting." Sue Ellen was smiling when she kissed him. She broke from his arms and ran out of the room.

One more minute there and I'd have been crying, King had thought. He watched the fire until it was cold, then went to bed.

The wagons were pulled up in front of the bunkhouse. Cook was on the seat of the chuckwagon waiting when King and Luke brought their bedrolls and extra clothes to the supply wagon. Henry Hastings was driving. "I thought you fellas was going to wait until tomorrow to start," he said.

Neither King nor Luke answered him. They threw their gear into the wagon and turned to mount their waiting horses. Henry shrugged his shoulders at their grim expressions and climbed on the wagon seat to start. The two men stayed silent during the days it took them to reach San Antonio. They did their camp tasks each night, then went to their beds without joining Cook and Henry at the campfire.

The wagons caught up with the herd the second morning. The riders waved as they passed. The herd was moving well. The cattle were tamer because of their months in Indian Creek basin. They were used to the riders, having learned that they could not outfox a determined man on a well-trained horse. That would make the whole drive easier. Only a few old mossyhorns gave the riders any real trouble. The drovers had orders to shoot any that continued to break for freedom.

King rode ahead of the wagons as they entered San Antonio. Luke rode beside him. The town was fairly quiet. There were no wagons gathered in the grove before the last long stretch of their journey west. They had probably left at the first sign of good weather. King hoped Clint and Rosita were all right.

When they reached the saloon King pulled Ranger to a halt. He turned to the men driving the wagons. "You know what we need in the way of supplies. Cook, get extra salt and coffee and flour in case we have to pay off some Indians. Buy all the .44 ammunition you can find. We'll meet you in front of the store about midday."

"We'll be done long afore that." Cook was plainly annoyed with King and Luke's continued ill humor.

"Meet us in the hotel restaurant then," King snapped. He turned his back to the wagons and tied Ranger's reins to the hitch rail. "Come on, Luke. I think a drink might make us both feel better." Luke tied his horse beside Ranger and followed King up the steps and through the double doors into the saloon.

King stepped up to the bar and ordered. "Pour us a couple of big ones, Slinger."

The man behind the bar placed two glasses in front of them and, reaching under the counter for a bottle, filled them to the brim. He leaned over the bar toward King and whispered, "Dale Billings is sitting over there at the corner table. He's been talking loud about what he's going to do when he catches you away from the protection of your drovers. He claims you back-shot his brother Hank."

"Much obliged for the warning, Slinger." King downed his drink without looking toward the corner where Billings was sitting. When he finished, he motioned for Luke to stay where he was and walked slowly over to the corner.

Billings was dealing cards. He concentrated on the cards in his hands and pretended not to notice King's approach.

The two men seated at the table with him were strangers to King. They were dressed in dark riding clothes identical to Billings' and wore holstered .44s, tied down.

King stood beside the table for a moment. He knew he could take Billings if it came to a fair draw, but the two other men wore their pieces like gunslingers. They might be ready to back up Billings' play.

"I hear you're looking for me, Billings."

Billings raised his head to look up at King. His face was pale. He rose to his feet, pushing his chair out of the way. "I wasn't exactly looking for you, blue-belly. The air was sure better in here before you showed up."

The insult was deliberate, calculated to anger King and make him rush his draw, giving Billings the advantage. "Well, I think maybe your nose doesn't work any better than your nerve, Billings."

King's left hand was tense, hovering just above his gun. His long fingers quivered slightly as though itching to move. He could hear chairs scraping and boots hitting the floor as men cleared a space behind him. The two men sitting at Billings' table eased their way off to the side, keeping their hands well away from their guns.

Billings stood alone. He knew King had outdrawn his brother Hank, who had enjoyed a reputation as a fast draw. Sweat ran down his forehead. His eyes were burning with hatred. He had to draw. His right hand moved slowly toward the butt of his .44. Suddenly his whole body tensed and he grabbed for the gun.

King's bullet caught him in the chest just as his gun cleared the holster. Billings' face went blank with surprise and then contorted in pain as he crumpled to the floor. King stepped forward to bend over the fallen man. He was dead when he reached him. The heavy slug had passed through his heart, killing him instantly.

Straightening up, the smoking Colt still in his hand, King turned toward the two men who had been playing cards with Billings. He looked at them questioningly, without speaking.

"We ain't got no quarrel with you, Sutherland," one of the men said. "We've got business over the border anyway." Nodding to his partner, the speaker led the way out the door.

Relieved, King holstered his gun and looked around to see Luke standing at the bar with a Colt in each hand. "I thought those two gents might want to back Billings' play," he said a little sheepishly, slipping his own gun into the holster at his side and placing the other on the bar. Slinger grabbed the gun and restored it to its hiding place under the bar.

"I sure appreciate y'all backing me. Slinger, will you see to Billings? I don't think he's got any folks left and his friends ain't the kind to worry about burying him."

"I'll see to it, King. His gun ought to be worth enough to get him buried." The bartender removed his apron and, calling to the Mexican swamper to keep the bar open, left the saloon by the rear door.

"Let's get out of here, Luke. I don't want to have to tangle with that sheriff Felton. Slinger will tell him what happened."

A man who had been standing at the far end of the bar came forward. "You needn't worry none about that four-flusher Felton. Them two marshals got him locked up in his own jail."

"You don't say." King didn't bother to hide his surprise. "What's he locked up for, do you know?"

"Seems one of them fellas from Riza that they hanged a few weeks ago told them marshals Felton was sending word to that Spaniard Alvaraz every time a stage or a wagon train left here without troopers along to guard it."

"So that's how they operated. I hadn't thought of that. Alvaraz sure would have needed someone to let him know what was going on. But a sheriff—that's downright hard to believe. Judge Wilkerson appointed him. He told me so himself. Boy, I'll bet he's hot."

"The whole town is hot. Felton will hang for sure. Them marshals let it be known how you and Luke Wilson helped them round up that murdering skunk Alvaraz. I'd say some folks are some kind of ashamed that they thought your brother was mixed up with Alvaraz's doings, Sutherland. Most of us old-timers hooted the stories anyhow."

"It's good of you to say that, Harris. You can take my word. Clint never robbed a stage or a wagon train. He never murdered anybody either." Brad Harris was a saloon bum and gossip. He always knew the facts on anything—for a free drink.

"Shucks, I knew that all along. No real Texan would do such a lowdown trick." Harris looked self-conscious and a little embarrassed. He had probably helped spread the stories about Clint and Alvaraz. He'd spread the new one just as fast. *Maybe by the time Dad gets out and around people again, folks will have forgotten the old stories completely,* King thought.

Paying for the bottle of whiskey on the bar, he pushed it toward Harris, and motioning to Luke to follow him, left the saloon. "Let's stop in at the jail and see how Race and Wingfield are doing before we leave town."

They left their horses where they stood and walked over to the jail. King felt elated at the turn of events. He couldn't help thinking about all his good fortune. The Sutherland name was clear in San Antonio. He felt as if a tremendous weight had been lifted from him. Life was good. He seemed to have everything going his way.

He and Sue Ellen would have a good life and he'd make a place for their children. The sadness of parting from Sue Ellen had left him. It was sweet to think of her waiting there at the ranch, but the challenge of driving a huge herd to the market in the north filled his mind. He knew he would dream of her every night on the trail, but his days would be full of the great adventure before him.

Wingfield rose from his chair behind the sheriff's desk as King and Luke entered the office. "Come on in here, boys," he said, extending his hand. "I've been expecting you two to come along soon."

"How are you, Wingfield? We heard about Sheriff Felton. It was a surprise, I'll tell you."

"It was a surprise around here too. That dude was some kin of those Billings boys. He got false references and came here as sheriff so he could bird-dog for Alvaraz. He slipped up on that last stage they hit. There was money in the strongbox, which he'd been notified about. What he didn't know was that he was the only man outside of Judge Wilkerson and Race and me that knew the money was there. It was too much of a coincidence that Alvaraz had passed up other stages and hit that one.

"When we faced Felton with what had happened at Riza, he broke down and talked. Course I kinda twisted the truth a little to get him to open up. I led him to believe that Alvaraz done some talking before he croaked, and Felton just caved in and told on himself."

"Wingfield, I just had a little fracas at the saloon with Dale Billings. He threw his gun and I had to shoot him."

"Is he dead?"

When King nodded, Wingfield kept on talking. "That figures. I heard he was loud-mouthing around about what all he was going to do when you showed up. His kind never does learn until they're dead. Forget about it, Sutherland. A fair fight's none of my mix." He waved his hand as though warding off a buzzing insect as he spoke.

"How's Race's arm, Wingfield?" Luke asked.

"It was broke pretty doggone bad, but Doc put it in a plaster cast. He claims it will heal straight. Race's as awkward as a day-old colt, but he can shoot as good with his left hand as he can with his right. I don't reckon anybody will kill him before he can use his arm again."

"Tell him we asked about him, will you?"

"I shore will. It's good of you to think about it. He'll appreciate it."

"We appreciate the help you and Race have been to us and to the town," King said. "How long will you stay here as acting sheriff?"

"Just until Judge Wilkerson gets a new sheriff and we hang Felton. I'd say maybe another week."

"Wingfield, when you come this way again, stop out at the ranch. You and Race will always be welcome there."

"That's real kind of you, Sutherland. We'll be down here again, no question about that. When we do, we'll make it our business to ride out to White Sun to see you."

Wingfield closed the office and walked between Luke and King as they returned to their horses. "When do you expect you'll get back from Abilene?"

"We're shooting for early summer. Luke's got a special reason to hurry back," King said, grinning at Luke.

"Yeah, I hear you. But I ain't the only one that hated to leave White Sun Ranch. You was dragging your feet all the way to town."

Wingfield laughed and slapped Luke's shoulder. "Don't let him rile you, boy. You all just take special care to get back in one piece. It ain't every man that's got a sweet girl waiting for him when he gets home. Good luck to you both."

The men shook hands and Luke and King hurried off to the hotel to meet Henry and Cook. It was late afternoon when the wagons reached the herd. The cattle were resting quietly, spread out over a wide area, knee-deep in grass. Several riders were lounging on the ground in a nearby grove of trees.

Cook and Henry pulled their wagons under the trees and unhitched the teams. Henry led the horses off to the creek while Cook lowered the wide tailgate at the rear of the chuckwagon and began to prepare a meal.

Neale rode up and dismounted. He had removed his coat while riding and tied it behind his saddle. "That sun gets hot out in the open. We'll roast before May," he said.

King walked over to join him. "How'd things go today?"

"It was like taking candy from a baby. Barring floods, Indians, and outlaws we ought to make it in a walk."

Luke spoke up from his position against the bole of a tree. "Don't forget stampedes and rustlers and four thousand other things that could go wrong."

"Don't you fellas go looking for trouble," Bill Ewell said. "We got a start on all the other trail herds and plenty of drovers to protect the herd. We can handle whatever comes."

"I know we can, Bill," King said. "You and Luke are the finest cattlemen I could ever find. We'll get through."

"Let's take a ride around the herd, Luke."

Leisurely riding close to the herd, they gradually made the circle. They spoke to each rider as they passed. When they got back in sight of camp, Cook waved to them and yelled "Come and get it!"

They joined the riders in a line behind the chuckwagon. Cook had prepared much more than standard range fare. He had cooked great slabs of steak, a huge pan of fried potatoes, and a dishpan piled high with cathead biscuits browned to a turn. There was a big pot of stewed peaches for dessert. The men piled food on their tin plates and ate with relish, washing the food down with cups of strong black coffee.

"Cook," King said as he wiped his plate with a piece of biscuit, "you've got a job for life."

Luke was chewing on his second piece of steak. "I've never eaten anything better in my life. I'll be fat by the time we get back to White Sun. Sallie won't even recognize me."

"You can bet you won't eat like this out on the trail, son," Bill said as he chuckled. "You'll be lucky to eat at all some days." Turning to Daniel Hastings, he said,

"Daniel, there'll be deer and wild turkey farther up the trail. Maybe you can do some hunting for us."

Daniel's face brightened. "If there's deer and turkey to be found, we'll eat like royalty. I can just taste what Cook could do to a big fat gobbler."

"As soon as we hit the timber you can hunt some every morning. It'll make our supplies last better. What do you say to that, Cook?"

"I've got plenty of supplies to last, but game would go down good. Beef can get almighty tiresome when you eat it every day."

"I expect Daniel will keep us in game, all we want. I might even join you some mornings, Daniel. I used to be pretty good in the woods. Luke was too," said King.

"That'd be fine, boss." Daniel stood up and stretched. "Let's some of us go watch them cows so the other boys can come in here and eat."

"How's the remuda handling, Neale?" Luke asked.

"They were a little frisky today, Luke. It took four men to keep them together, even using the *vaqueros*."

"I'll take first watch tonight. Maybe I can calm them down a little." Luke untied his horse and led him a few steps away from the camp, then mounted and rode out toward the horse herd.

King sat where he was and smoked as the other men came in and got their meals. They talked and joked as they ate, happy to be on the trail. When they finished eating, Jim and Billy helped Cook clean up. The other men left the fire one by one to unroll their blankets under the trees.

The herd moved along easily the first day. They made camp about ten miles north of San Antonio in another grove of trees. There was an abundance of dried grass for the cattle, and a deep creek provided water.

Luke and the men helping him had trouble keeping the remuda bunched and moving along with the herd. The horses were strong and fresh and they didn't like walking beside the cattle. By noon, Juan and Eduardo had to drop back to help keep them together. It was dark before Luke and the *vaqueros* rode into camp. Their faces were dirty and their clothes were covered in dust.

Ben Hastings ran to take their horses' bridles. "You fellas go on and eat, I'll take care of your horses."

"Bless you, boy," Luke said. "That bunch of ornery cayuses just about worked me to death today." He wiped the sweat from his face with a bandanna. "I think they'll hold now. They've run some of the edge off. A few days of steady walking will calm them down."

"Fill your plate and bring it over here, Luke," King called to him from his seat beside the creek. "Those horses will be all right now. We'll soon be working them so hard they'll be glad to take it easy."

"I know. They just had to show off a little, I reckon. They've got it out of their systems now."

Luke sat down on a hummock of grass near King and wolfed down his food. Some men carried some jerky or bacon and biscuits left from breakfast in their saddlebags to eat on the run, as the chuckwagon never set up for a noonday meal on the trail.

"I want you to ride point starting tomorrow, Luke. Let Juan and Eduardo and Roy Jerdone keep the horses together. I need you to help me keep the herd moving right."

"Heck, it ain't no problem to stay on the trail. We've gotta bear a little east from here. But if we can keep the Cross Timbers country to our left and head almost due north, we'll hit the Colorado near Austin."

"We'll reach the Colorado in about two weeks. The last camp will be dry, but the water's good most places this time of year and there should be plenty of grass, at least until we cross the Brazos. There may be plenty even then, this time of year."

"There's more than a hundred miles of heavy timber between the Brazos and the Red River. Feed could be short for the cattle. That section will take us a little less than two weeks if we're lucky. If we push through there, we can rest the herd at Whitestone, just after we cross the Red. There's bound to be good grass there."

"I know you'd rather stay with the horses, Luke, but I'd still feel better with you up front. Get Daniel Hastings to ride with you. He's a natural scout. He can ride ahead and look over the ground for the next day's drive so we'll always know what we're facing."

"That sounds good to me, but I'd thought you'd want Bill Ewell riding out front." Luke looked over at King.

"Bill would be just as good riding point as far as the work goes, I know that. But I'd just plain feel better to have you up there. This herd means almost as much to you as it does to me."

"I hadn't thought of it exactly like that, but I reckon you're about right." Luke raised himself upright. "I'm going to wash off some of this trail dust and crawl in my blankets. I'll take the herd out in the morning."

King woke to the sound of the men moving the herd. He left his blankets and stepped in the open to watch. The cattle were spread out over a wide, flat area. The trail led up a long incline so most of the cattle were visible from where he stood. Luke and Daniel were riding point with the herd spread out in a huge triangle behind them.

The dark mottled bodies of the cattle jostled and moved along like a river. Their horns flashed black and gray and white in the rising sun. King could hear them click and crash together over the rumble of their hooves and the yells of the riders.

He raised his hand and waved to Juan and Eduardo as they razed the remuda out to one side of the herd. The other riders were spaced along the broad rear of the cattle, almost pushing them with their horses. Now and then a carbine or .44 would crack as the men were forced to kill newborn calves too slow to keep up with the herd.

If the weather holds, we'll make good time for the next few weeks at least, King thought. Shaking himself out of the spell of watching the herd, he hurried back to roll up his blankets and get to the campfire for breakfast.

"I figured you had done died in yore sleep," Cook grumbled as King filled his plate. "Since all them hogs is gone out with the herd, I'll cook you up some eggs. I got three hid in the wagon."

"I'll sure eat them. It'll be a long time until we get any again."

"I reckon I know some folks up trail that will sell me some eggs and maybe some apples. If they've got some left since last fall. We gonna be almighty tired of beef and beans by that time. They might even have a few dried-up potatoes left in their cellar."

King ate quickly, watching Cook pack up his gear. He was amazed at the efficiency of the tough old man. A good cook was a treasure on a trail drive. The men couldn't stand to work from daylight to dark for long unless they had plenty of good food.

King spent his days riding, filling in where he was needed. He had decided to keep five riders with the herd, even when they were bedded down at night, and he took his turn riding night guard with the others. The weather stayed clear until they reached Austin, but it was too early in the year to expect good weather to hold all the way. King was confident they could survive anything short of a blizzard without too much hardship.

Chapter Eight

Luke led the herd west around the town and held them on a long slope near the river. The Colorado was in flood. Instead of flowing, the water writhed and rolled. The river was out of its banks in low places, red with mud picked up by the rushing water. Here and there a log or a whole tree bobbed in and out of its surface.

"I'll be a son of a gun. Will you look at that?" King said. "Will we have to wait for that mess to go down?"

Luke sat his horse beside him. "Heck, no. We'd be here a week or more. We'll hold the herd here tonight and take them over at first light tomorrow. Them old mossyhorns can swim like ducks. This place is wide enough to get them across safe. It's a good two miles down before the banks get steep again. I'll take the herd in just beside those trees over there and the boys can push 'em hard. The current might move some of them downstream, but we'll get most of them across quick."

"I'll take the *vaqueros* and ride the downstream side," King said. "Ranger's bigger than most of the horses and he can fight the current. Those men can't be matched on a horse. We'll hold the herd in the open space."

Luke shook his head. "That's shore dangerous business. You could get yourself pushed downstream and trapped by those high banks. You'd be better off to lose a few of these cows if it comes to it."

"I don't expect to lose even one if I can help it." King's voice had a harsh edge to it.

"Be it on your head then. I can't stop you." Luke turned his horse away from King and walked it back to where Cook was setting up camp.

King rode into town. The streets and sidewalks were crowded with people. He noticed new houses and new places of business here and there. Dismounting in front of the biggest store, he tied Ranger and went inside.

People crowded around on the store porch. He saw men dressed in buckskin, obviously trappers, and cattlemen dressed the same as he and his men. Some were undoubtedly farmers or settlers on their way west. The lure of free land and a new start brought families that would fill up the country.

The storekeeper seemed extremely glad to see King. "I got word your herd was in sight of town, down toward the river. Are there many more herds coming up behind you?"

The man was a stranger to King, but he liked him on sight. "There'll be more cows up the trail than you can count this year. I'm hoping I got the jump on them. Normal time to start would be next month. We just happened to be able to get our herd ready during the winter and could move as soon as the weather began to warm up."

"You're right there, young fella. I hate to tell you, but you're bound to hit some weather soon. Winter ain't completely finished with us yet, and that's a fact. I'd say you should look for it in the next few days."

"My name is Dan Chandler," he said, holding his hand across the counter to King. "What's your handle?"

"I'm Kingsley Sutherland from the Blanco Sol Ranch south of San Antonio." King reached over to shake hands with the storekeeper.

"Whew! You've come a long way already. Have you been up the trail before?"

"No, I haven't, but I've got a trail boss that knows the country. We'll find our way all right."

"If you get your herd across the Colorado, you've still got weeks of driving ahead of you. I heard there's been some Indian trouble over in Baxter Springs. You might have to fight for your herd before you're through."

"We'll handle Indians if we have to," King said. "Could you fill this order of supplies and have it ready for my cook to pick up in the morning? We'll be taking the herd across the river early tomorrow."

"You'd be much safer if you could wait a few days. That river is a real monster right now."

"If I sit here and wait for it to go down, it might rain again, or there'll be other herds pushing me from behind. I want to be the first to reach Abilene this year."

"You'll make a mint if you do that. I heard the other day that cattle prices are high. McCoy's supposed to be offering ten dollars a head for beef."

"Ten dollars! He'll have every cow in Texas running up that trail at that price." King was filled with excitement. If he could get the herd to Abilene intact, it would bring over twenty thousand dollars—barring a disaster. *I'll get them there*, he resolved. *It will bring us a fortune. I'll comb the brakes and make a drive every year for that kind of money.*

He said goodbye to Chandler and left the store, riding out of town without visiting the saloon. He was worried that if he stayed away too long, Windy Mason and Matt Horn might decide to ride in. If they got started drinking, he might have to leave them behind, and they were needed.

Everyone was in camp when King returned except Roy and Ben, who were tending the horses, and two men who were watching the herd. He addressed the group around the fire. "The storekeeper in town thinks there's other herds coming along right behind us. He warned me of Indian trouble ahead, too."

"It would take a lot of Indians to give twenty well-armed men any trouble," Neale said.

"That's for sure," said Bill Ewell. "Mostly, redskins just

beg for food and a few cows to slaughter. They ain't armed good enough to tackle big outfits like us."

"I purely hope you're right, Bill." King walked over near the men and took his bedroll out of the pile of bedding. "What worries me is the weather. The sky has looked sort of a dull gray for the last couple of days. I keep thinking I can smell rain or snow or some kind of falling weather. You boys go on and get some sleep, but nobody leave camp. You'll be needed at first light." King was careful to look straight at Windy and Matt as he spoke. Both riders looked guilty as they left the fire. It was obvious to King that they had been planning to go into town. They would probably sneak out of camp as soon as everyone else was asleep.

It was still dark the next morning when King felt someone shake his shoulder. Luke was leaning over him. "Roll out, old man. Get you some grub so we can make an early start."

By the time the riders had eaten their breakfast, the cattle were beginning to stand up and move about. The gray sky had lightened a little when Juan led the horses into camp. The men grabbed their gear and caught the horses they planned to use for the day. When they finished, there were two extra horses.

"Where's Windy and Matt?" King asked.

Bill Fwell stepped up to answer for his men. "I'll be darned if those two sorry so-and-sos didn't leave camp, King—after you said not to. I warned them you wouldn't stand for it."

"You're dead right there, Bill. As far as I'm concerned, those two boys are stuck right here."

"I can't fault you none for that, boss. They was warned. Nobody here's got time to be babysitting two grown men."

"Let's get moving," Luke said. "Daniel, you'll be needed behind the herd today. Roy, you and Ben take the horses across first. I'll point the herd and you boys drive them cows into that water running. Keep yourselves as clear as you can. If you fall in, you're a goner in that flood."

Ben and Roy had the remuda bunched and the horses headed into the river. They had no fear of water normally, but the roaring flood frightened them and made them skittish. They poured down the slope at a trot, snorting and tossing their heads. The yelling riders drove them over the sloping bank. Water splashed high as they pounded into the shallows.

By the time most of the horses were off the bank, the leaders were in deep water, swimming for the other side. Roy and Ben rode their horses in after them, yelling and shooting their pistols into the air to keep the herd moving. The horses' heads glistened above the surface of the water. It was all over in minutes. The horses heaved themselves out of the water and ran up the far bank, still well bunched. They trotted a few hundred yards and stopped to graze.

King relaxed a little after seeing the ease with which the horses crossed. With a little luck the cattle would make it across just as easily. He turned Ranger away from the river. He wanted to work his way around beside the cattle. The longhorns were on their feet now and milling about. Luke stood his horse between the herd and the river, waiting for all the riders to get in position.

Juan, Eduardo, and King took their places on the down-river side of the herd. Luke would lead the point downhill to the upper edge of the open area and hit the water there. The drovers would have to push the herd to a run to get them across before the current took them too far down the river. The high banks on the far side would block them if they drifted too far downstream; they would get tired from swimming, and the wild water would drown them before they could find another place to get out of the water.

Swinging a rope in a wide loop, Luke rode across in front of the herd. He dropped the loop around the horns of a huge bull. He spun his horse toward the river and pulled the old mossyhorn after him. At that moment the nervous cattle started to run. The herd fell in behind the bull, making a long narrow triangle pointed toward Luke's running horse. The riders were yelling at the top of their voices and shooting their guns into the air.

The cattle had no fear of the water. Luke's horse hit the shallows, sending yellow sheets of water flying. The big old bull was running on his own. The herd pushed the frontrunners into the swirling red water. Luke's horse began to swim. King could see only Luke's head and shoulders and his horse's head. His heart almost stopped when the horse seemed to falter for a moment. Then Luke pulled the horse's head up and swam him straight for the far bank.

Cattle were pouring down the long slope, running flat out. The sound of their hooves hitting the earth became an enveloping thunder. Dust made it hard to see the front of the herd any longer. The *vaqueros* helped King push the cattle upriver as they ran pell-mell for the bank. Their horns crackled and boomed against each other, adding to the noise of their hooves.

When King reached the near bank, Juan was in the water in front of him. His horse was swimming. He swiftly reloaded his pistol and continued to yell and fire in the air. The herd strung out across the river. The cattle swam strongly and held the pattern it would take to get them across safely.

King pushed Ranger into the deep water. The great horse swam easily against the swift current. He showed no fear of the longhorns, working in close to hold them in line. King could no longer hear the thundering sound of the cattle. Either they were all in the water or the sound had deafened him. Cattle passed him. The racing current carried them to a point on the far bank that was almost half a mile from where they entered the water.

Here and there small groups of cattle broke away from the herd to let the current take them. King and the *vaqueros* swam their horses back and forth, forcing the cattle to stay with the herd. Daniel and Billy and the other riders came into the water with them. The cattle had followed the leaders like sheep. All that remained for the riders to do was keep them moving toward the other bank.

Suddenly Daniel's horse went under in the racing current and Daniel bobbed to the surface, sputtering. He floated right beside a big steer that swam along with his horns held high. King turned Ranger downstream to get below him. The current moved Daniel and the steer closer together. The man's efforts to swim were almost useless in the swift current.

King looped his wet rope, ready to throw it to Daniel as soon as he could get close enough. The swirling water spun Daniel around and he saw Ranger a second before he reached him. He lunged for the rope and grabbed it in one hand.

Tying the rope around the pommel of his saddle, King pulled with both hands. One of the horns of the big steer snagged Daniel's shoulder as he passed him. King saw blood cover the sleeve of his jacket. His right arm fell limp.

King swam Ranger closer and pulled at the rope at the same time. "Here, Daniel," he yelled, almost in the man's ear. "Climb up behind me. Use your left hand to hold on."

Daniel struggled up behind King's saddle and clung to his waist. Ranger took no notice of the increased weight on his back. King turned him back toward the bank. Ranger breasted the current with steady strokes of his powerful legs. When he reached shallow water, his head jerked high and his dripping shoulders left the water as he lunged up the bank.

Riding straight for the campsite where Cook was packing the wagons, King yelled, "Help me get him on the ground!"

Cook came running to grab Daniel as he slid off the horse's back. "What in thunder happened to him? Has he been shot?" He turned Daniel on his side and saw the long gash in Daniel's shoulder. Blood had mingled with the water in his jacket and it looked as though he had bled a terrible amount.

"The horn of a big old bull struck his shoulder and cut him. He hasn't lost as much blood as it looks, but he's lost enough. Get the medicine box."

Daniel moaned as King cut and pulled his wet jacket and shirt away from the gaping wound. The tip of the steer's horn had sliced Daniel's shoulder in a long curve from his arm to the middle of his back.

Cook came running with the medicine box, placing it at King's side. "Get me some blankets, Cook," King said. "He feels frozen."

King grabbed the bottle of carbolic and poured it over the

wound. Daniel didn't flinch, he had fainted with the pain and loss of blood.

The wound looked like some of the saber cuts King had seen during the war. He took a needle from the box and threaded it with coarse black thread. He had seen wounds sewn up before but he had never done it himself, not even on a horse or cow. But he knew this had to be done. The cut was too deep to leave open.

He pushed the needle into the pale skin of Daniel's back at one end of the cut. The feeling of the needle moving through flesh was horrible to King. He pulled the thread tight and tied it off. It took more than twenty stitches to close the cut to his satisfaction. He tied the last one with hands covered with blood and sweat and straightened up.

"Can you bandage it and get him dry and warm?" he asked Cook in a shaky voice.

Cook nodded and took King's place beside Daniel. King stumbled away from the camp. He stopped to lean weakly against a tree trunk. He couldn't stop shaking. The nausea that had threatened to overcome him at the feel of the first stitch in Daniel's shoulder welled up into his throat, and he retched on the ground.

Daniel lay sleeping near a blazing fire, all wrapped up in blankets, when King returned to the camp. His color had improved dramatically.

"Is there any coffee left?"

"I made a new pot. Here you go, boss. I put some red-eye in it. Figured you might be wanting it."

He passed a tin cup filled with the steaming liquid to King. "I got a few drops down Daniel. If he don't wake up quick I'll make him a bed in the wagon."

"Go ahead and do that anyway, Cook. He lost a lot of blood. He'll be too weak to ride for a few days at least."

"I kin put him in the supply wagon. We got to git moving. I'll be lucky to ketch up to the herd by night."

"We'll catch up. Luke's going to hold the cattle a few miles from the river. Some of the boys will be back here to help get the wagons across the river."

"I got to get over to Austin first. Some fresh supplies would taste good."

"You go ahead to town, I'll wait here with Daniel."

Refilling his coffee cup, King sat down beside the fire and watched Daniel's face. He felt satisfied the boy would be all right.

Neale and Henry Hastings rode into the camp. Jim and Billy had come back with them to help get the wagons across the river. Neale and Henry jumped off their horses and ran to Daniel.

"What happened?" Neale asked, kneeling beside his brother. His face paled.

"He fell off his horse in the river. A longhorn cut a slice in his shoulder. It was right bad. He fainted from the shock, I think."

"He looks so washed out," Henry said, almost whispering, in a voice filled with fear.

"He lost a lot of blood. I had to sew his shoulder up."

"I didn't know you could do that."

"I didn't either, but it had to be done. Blood was pouring out of him. It was the only way I knew to stop it. Let's go cut a couple of poles so we can make a stretcher to get him in the wagon."

When Cook returned with the supplies, they moved the wagons across the river without mishap. It was only about three miles to where Luke had the herd bedded down.

King was elated. They hadn't lost a single head of cattle in one of the most dangerous river crossings on the trail. They'd made a good start. They were short three riders, with Windy and Matt gone and Daniel injured, but the next few weeks would be fairly easy on the cattle and the Brazos would be easy to cross compared to the Colorado.

The sky clouded over in the early afternoon and the riders got cold in their damp clothes. The men huddled close to the campfire as they ate their supper. The wind was picking up and blowing from the north instead of the usual southwest.

"Two riders coming in, boss." Charlie Bull called out.

Windy Mason and Matt Horn approached, riding slowly. Horn rode close to Mason, holding him in the saddle. Both men seemed unsteady and their eyes showed they'd had too much to drink. They stopped their horses near the chuckwagon and dismounted. Horn continued to support Mason as they approached the fire.

"Sorry we're so late, boss." Horn said.

King lay his plate on the ground beside him and rose to his feet. "Horn, I gave you a direct order not to leave camp. You and Mason are through here. Get some supper, then clear out of my camp."

"Aw, boss. We missed one lousy day. It ain't fair not to let a man have a little time off, as hard as we work."

"You knew what the deal was when we left Blanco Sol. I don't want riders that can't follow orders."

"Ain't no call for you to be so doggone high and mighty," Windy yelled at King, his voice thick and slurred with drink.

"My orders were plain enough. Now get some food in you and get out of my camp. Make sure you're riding your own horses when you leave." King turned his back on them and left the campfire to stand in the trees nearby.

Horn and Mason filled their plates and sat down beside the campfire to eat. Mason continued to grumble drunkenly about people who thought they were better than poor drovers. Both men straightened up quickly after they ate and drank several cups of coffee, but Matt Horn's usually pleasant face was ugly with anger. He continued to mutter bitter comments to Mason.

Horn suddenly raised his voice and yelled at King's back, "You're nothing but a lowdown blue-coat traitor. I'll fix you for this."

King ignored him. He continued to stand with one shoulder against the bole of a tree. His back was turned to the campfire.

Matt Horn stood up and yanked his gun from its holster.

"Hey, hold on there!" Luke ran up to the fire to grab for Horn's arm.

"Keep your mouth out of this, Wilson. Nobody fires me."

"King Sutherland just did. Now you and Windy get your possibles out of the wagon and leave this camp." Luke stepped back and dropped his hand near his gun. His body was crouched down a little. He was ready to draw.

"You make me sick, Wilson. You'd kiss that high-toned son-of-a-gun's behind." Horn turned his gun on Luke as he spoke.

Luke's hand flashed to his gun as Horn fired. Horn's shot merely skimmed Luke's left coat sleeve. The crash of his gun came an instant after Horn's. The bullet caught Horn's left eye and blew away part of his forehead. His body seemed to fold up as he fell to the ground.

Luke turned his gun on Windy Mason. "Are you ready to try me?" His words sounded like a snarl. He was still standing in a crouch, his gun ready.

"I ain't drunk enough to try to draw when you've got the drop on me." Mason stood up carefully. He appeared to be cold sober. His face flushed with anger, but he held his hands almost straight out from his sides, well away from his gun.

"Get your horse and your bedroll and ride out of here. We'll plant your friend. Take his horse with you."

Mason sidled past Luke and grabbed his bedroll out of the back of the supply wagon. He ran to mount his horse and, holding Horn's horse by the reins, galloped to the south.

Luke holstered his gun and stalked away from the fire. He didn't speak. King stood over Horn's body. He had run back to the campfire when the first shot rang out, but everything had happened so fast that it was all over by the time that he reached Luke's side.

Bill Ewell stood looking down at Horn's body with a sad expression. "Matt here asked for a shooting and he got it, King. The darn fool set out to shoot you in the back. Then he tried to take on Luke Wilson. He should have known better to start with. He was a stupid drunk." Bill turned on his heel and walked over to stare into the fire.

King shook his head helplessly. "I'm so sorry, Bill. I never thought firing those boys would cause gunplay."

"It ain't any of your fault, King. Horn always got a little

crazy when he was drunk. Luke called him and Horn had the drop on Luke. He never even went for his gun until Horn fired."

"That's more than once Luke Wilson has shot a man on my account. It's a shame what liquor can do to a good man."

Willis Hastings and another cowhand picked up Matt Horn's body and carried him away from the campfire. His bloody head lolled back limply as the men lifted him. King shuddered at the sight. It made him feel cold with dread. One man was dead and another seriously hurt. He wondered how many of them would finish the drive.

The riders seemed to draw closer to each other the next few days. There was no joking or card playing around the campfire after supper. The men just sat and talked, keeping their voices low. The shock of Horn's death seemed to make them crave comradeship.

The herd reached the Brazos over a week ahead of schedule. They crossed easily. King took the next few days slowly, letting the cattle graze some every day. When they reached the heavily timbered country between the Brazos and the Red River, they would have to manage on scant grass.

The weather turned bitterly cold. The men bundled up in extra shirts under their jackets. Several made makeshift ponchos by cutting head holes out of extra blankets. They were grateful for the protection from the wind offered by the trees.

Keeping the cattle together became difficult. They were strung out along a narrow trail only two or three dozen abreast. Any strays were hard to recover in the brush. Men and horses endured constant scratching and whipping by branches and briars as they crashed through the woods. The riders' clothes and boots became tattered and torn. By the time the timber opened up, they all looked like ragamuffins.

When the herd reached the Red River, sleet was falling. The riders hunched over their saddlehorns, nearly frozen. Their long slickers made them look like ghosts. The river was flowing normally. It took the better part of a day to work the entire herd and the horse remuda across.

Cook built two big fires at the campsite. The riders huddled between them, holding their plates with fingers racked by pain as they thawed in the blazing heat. The men cursed the ice and as soon as they could swallow their food they grabbed their bedrolls and bundled up close together under the wagons. Jim and Billy rigged a long tarp between the wagons. It provided shelter from at least part of the driving rain and sleet.

King spent a cold and miserable night, shivering until the warmth of his blankets finally lulled him to sleep. He woke just before dawn, wet and freezing again. His slicker had kept the water from the top of his blankets, but water had run along the ground to soak his shoulders.

"Blast it all anyway," he muttered. He pulled his boots from under his blankets and yanked them onto his feet. Moving to keep warm, he found more wood, built up the fire, and filled the coffeepot. As soon as he sat down by the fire, Luke joined him.

"Nasty night," he said. "I hate to be cold."

"How long to the trading post?" asked King.

"I'm gonna guess it's about more ten miles. I'd say it's another whole day."

"As soon as we eat, let's push along. The outfit could sure use a day's rest. Barring trouble, we'll get to the trading post before dark. We'll rest this evening and most of the day tomorrow. That'll give everybody a chance to relax a few hours. They might even be able to get dry and warm."

"That's a good idea, King. Everybody's tail is dragging. Shivering takes more energy than riding. It looks like things are going to clear up today, though."

"I think you're right about that. I sure hope so. It must be some time into April. You'd think bad weather should be over."

"This ought to be the last of it," Luke said, and King hoped he was right.

Chapter Nine

Peaple filled the trading post. A cluster of wagons sat in the open area beside the store. Twenty or more horses stood tied at hitch rails along the short street. Several Indians stood on one side of the long front porch, their faces showing no expression as they stared at the riders.

Luke and King rode in together. They entered the store and worked their way through the stacks of supplies and trade goods and people to reach the counter. The trading post catered to Indians and white men alike. Great bundles of furs stacked against one wall gave evidence of the Indians and trappers trading there.

The trader hailed them cheerily. "You boys driving that big herd that came in today?"

"What's left of us," King said. "I'm Sutherland. My friend here is Luke Wilson."

"My name is Ed Dawson and you fellas sure are a welcome sight. You're driving through early. Ain't nobody ahead of you on this route."

"That's what we figured on. How's things up ahead of us?"

"I'd say you're too early for buffalo, which is a blessing. The Indians have caused some trouble lately though. There's a big chief of the Kiowa and a band of about fifty redskins that have been running around shooting up small wagon trains and burning settlers out. Folks tell me that chief was

167

responsible for a massacre up to Baxter Springs last fall. From all I can hear, he's mean and ready to fight if you're weak, but smart enough to leave you alone if you can show plenty of firepower."

"We've got near twenty riders and we're all well armed."

"I'd advise you to parley with him if he comes to your camp. Take some extra coffee and tobacco along. Give him that as a gift and let him have a look at your guns."

"I'm obliged for your advice, Dawson. Fill out this list for me, will you? Double the tobacco, coffee, and ammunition we've got listed on there. My supply wagon will be in short-ly to pick them up."

"Whew! You feed your men good, don't you? I loaded up on supplies, figuring on the traffic being heavy on the trail this year, but if they all feed like this, I'm sure going to be short on stock."

"Dawson, the trail will be thick with outfits in a few weeks. I'd advise you to send for more supplies right now if you can. The herds will be here. Cattlemen are almost starv-ing in Texas. I just hope McCoy will be able to handle the cattle that are coming up this trail in a few weeks."

"You've given me an idea, Sutherland. I'm gonna send my wagons over to Fort Smith for more goods. It might look like I've got a lot, but a few big orders like yours will make a ter-rible hole in them."

"Maybe we'll all make some money this year. Have you heard anything about what McCoy is paying for cows?"

"I understand his top price last year was eight dollars a head. If you're one of the first up there this year, you should get more."

"That would make me happy," King said. "We'll probably see you in a few weeks, Dawson."

"You take care now, boys."

The riders had cleaned themselves up and put on the cleanest clothes they owned when King and Luke returned to the camp.

"You dudes going somewhere special?" Luke asked the group.

Willis hitched his belt as he stood up. "Them cows ain't going anywhere. They're too tired and hungry to do anything but stay out there in that grass and eat. We want to ride in to Dawson's for a drink."

"King and I will ride guard. You boys go ahead in. Take care to be back here sober by morning, though."

The riders tore out of camp whooping and yelling. King chuckled as he watched them mount their houses and gallop off toward the post.

"I hope you're right in letting them go, Luke," he said, filling his cup from the coffeepot.

"After what happened with Horn, I think we can depend on them. I'm not going to worry about it."

King was walking toward the wagon. "I'm going to talk to Daniel. I'll be along in a minute or two."

Daniel sat in the wagon, propped up against some sacks. "Hey there, boss," he said, grinning as King stuck his head over the tailgate. "Climb on in here and set a spell. I can move my feet."

"I'll stand here. How are you feeling?"

"I'm much better than my brothers want to think I am. Neale took the stitches out of my shoulder and said it's healing fine. I been riding a little the last few days."

"You take it slow. Can you move your arm all right?"

"I sure can. It's a little stiff, but it seems to be all right."

"Give it plenty of time to heal. You can ride the wagon some and help Cook. The trail's pretty easy from now on in. At least, it will be as soon as we cross the Arkansas. We can handle the cattle fine without you." King jumped down from the wagon and, catching up Ranger's reins, mounted and rode out to help Luke watch the herd.

The weather improved as the days passed. It was getting late in April and they were well over the halfway mark to Abilene. There was less grass for the cattle and they had to make dry camp frequently. Cook carried two barrels of water strapped to the sides of the chuckwagon. He had rigged up a canvas under both wagons and the men gathered up any wood they found and threw it in one of them so they could make fires for cooking and to keep warm. They also packed the back of the supply wagon with firewood.

Daniel soon got back on his feet and rode scout in front of the herd. He left before the herd moved in the mornings and came back to spell Luke at point around noon with a camp-site already picked out for that night. King came to depend on his sharp eyes and hunting instinct to keep the herd traveling the easiest route.

One morning, as the riders were finishing breakfast, Daniel rode into camp yelling, "Indians up ahead. Get your rifles ready." He jumped to the ground before his horse slid to a complete stop. "It's a big bunch—it may be them Kiowas."

The men ran to their saddles to grab their rifles. Willis dashed toward the herd to warn the drovers riding guard and to tell the *vaqueros* to bring the remuda nearer to camp.

"Stand easy, boys," King said. "Keep near the wagons so you can take cover if any shooting starts, but don't you start anything. I'm going to try to talk us out of this."

King and Luke stepped out in the open to watch the Indians approach. There appeared to be around thirty in the group, their lean brown bodies gleaming in the sun. They rode ragged, thin, wild-looking ponies, still shaggy with their winter coats. Their long black hair was held back by colorful bandannas tied around their dark foreheads.

As the men came closer, King thought they were the embodiment of wildness. Their faces were cruel and hard-looking. Most carried lances in their hands and bows slung over their shoulders. He saw only a few armed with rifles.

The foremost Indian had to be the chief Dawson had told him about. His carriage was erect, almost stiff. When he rode close to the campfire, King could see hatred and some-thing like contempt in his piercing black eyes. He stood his ground and stared back at the chief.

"Get Charlie Bull up here, Luke. He speaks Kiowa, I think that's what his folks were." He shifted the weight of the buffalo gun he held into the crook of his arm, keeping the muzzle pointed at the ground.

Charlie came up to stand at King's right. Luke stepped forward to take the place on his left. "Go talk to him, Charlie. Tell him I'll give them beef, salt, coffee, and tobacco, if you have to. But tell him we'll kill him and all of his men if he gives us any trouble."

Charlie Bull stepped out toward the mounted Indian. King could see a faint similarity in the shape of the two men. The cruelty in the chief's face made it hard for him to believe that Charlie came from the same race.

The harsh voice of the Indian barked out at Charlie. King couldn't understand any of the words, but the meaning was plain. Charlie answered in the same tone. His voice sound foreign and brutal in the Indian tongue.

The chief waved his hands and yelled angrily at Charlie, pointing at the wagons.

Charlie turned and came back to King. "Boss, he says he wants twenty head of beef and plenty of supplies and ammunition."

King looked up at the mounted Indian and caught his eye. He shook his head to indicate he wouldn't agree to his demands. The Indian immediately shook his rifle in the air and yelled something. Charlie Bull walked back to the Indian and spoke to him harshly, holding up his fingers to indicate what King would agree to give.

The Indian yelled at Charlie for a few more minutes, then nodded his head in agreement. Charlie came back to King. "He'll take the supplies, boss. I agreed he could have ten cows. He says his village is starving."

"I don't like it, Charlie, but I don't reckon ten cows will kill us. It's nothing but plain old robbery. Help Cook bring one sack each of flour, coffee, and salt. Bring that long box of tobacco."

The Indians piled the bags of supplies in front of them on their saddles, holding them against their lean bellies with one arm. The leader stared at King and the heavily armed riders for a moment, then yanked his pony around, scattering the men behind him as he rode through.

"You men stay in a group and ride down there to see they don't cut out but ten cows," King ordered.

"Blasted lowdown robbers," Luke said bitterly. "We fight them longhorns all the way from south Texas and them redskins just waltz in and steal them. We could have took them braves easy. They didn't have hardly any guns, and them they had looked like they might have been made in the Revolution."

"Let it go, Luke. It's cheap at the price. We haven't got time to be fighting Indians. They'll stampede the herd if we start anything, anyway."

Daniel or another of the men spotted Indians again several times before they reached Abilene, but no more rode into camp. The riders guarded the herd day and night.

Chapter Ten

A man rode out to meet the herd as they approached Abilene. A small, slim fellow, he looked nervous. His face was covered with a heavy beard and he was dressed in eastern clothing, making him appear out of place among the riders. He rode up to King and stuck out his hand.

"I'm Joseph McCoy. Your scout pointed you out to me."

"I'm glad to meet you, Mr. McCoy. I'm Kingsley Sutherland from the Blanco Sol Ranch south of San Antonio, Texas."

"Yours is the first herd up the trail this year," McCoy said. "You and your boys look like you had to crawl part of the way." He looked around at the rugged, trail-worn drovers. Some were bearded; they were all dirty, including King.

"No, McCoy, we didn't have to crawl any, but we shore ran most of the way."

McCoy laughed. Looking around at the herd, he asked, "How many of these cows do you have?

"A few more than twenty-two hundred head, by my guess. They're in good condition, too. What are you paying this year?"

"I ended up last year paying eight dollars a head. I guess I could start there this year."

"That's not enough. I'm days ahead of another herd and my cattle are big and fairly fat."

173

"How much do you want?"

"I figure they ought to go for around twelve dollars."

"Can't go that high. I'll give you ten—and not a penny more. You sure can't take them anywhere else."

"I reckon you've got me there, McCoy. I'll take the ten dollars and thank you for it. Give me about fifteen hundred in cash and a draft on the Cattleman's Bank for the difference. I'll pick it up after we make the count."

"There's a hotel over there in that new building. You and your drovers might want to get a room so you can clean up, Sutherland."

"You own the hotel too, McCoy?" King asked.

"I do, and the saloon and the store. Just about everything you can see." McCoy puffed himself up with pride in his business efforts.

"Is that a fact? Well, we've got some work to do. I'll see you later." King shook McCoy's hand again and turned Ranger toward the herd. The riders made short work of rousting the cattle into McCoy's fenced areas. When the herd reached the pens, McCoy's men pitched in to help make the count as the cattle entered the gates.

Twenty-three thousand, two hundred and sixty dollars for less than a year's work. It seemed unreal to King. He had lived with his dream for so long, it was hard for him to believe he had actually achieved what he set out to do. He went to McCoy's office to pick up his money, and then he and the riders went back out of town to the wagons.

As tired as they were, every man hurried through his supper, then dashed to the creek to clean himself up and change his clothes.

"Did you get some cash for the boys, King?" Luke asked.

"You bet I did. I know how they feel. It'll take two or three days of bucking the tiger for them to get this out of their systems. Are you going into town with them?"

"I sort of figured on it. How about you?"

"I guess it wouldn't seem very friendly if I didn't. I want to head for home as soon as I can, though," King said.

"Maybe we can drag them back here tonight."

"Nah, let them have one night. I might just stay here to-night and guard the wagons and horses while you go in with them and I'll go in tomorrow night. Maybe we can get them back here early enough then to start for home in one more day."

"We can try. There's more than whiskey to keep them here, though. One of McCoy's riders said there was a Monte game in a back room in McCoy's hotel that most riders like to try. He's got girls there too." Luke sounded a little interested himself.

"We'll be lucky if we get those drovers out of this town in less than a week. I'm going to give each man twenty dollars and hold their pay until we get back to Santone."

"That might hold them down a little. I'll go talk to them. They don't want to get left up here, I know that."

The men returned to the campfire bathed and dressed in their cleanest, least ragged clothes. Bill Ewell came up to stand before King with his hat in his hand. "We need some money, boss. Ain't anybody here got as much as fifty cents in his pocket."

"Bill, I got a little cash from McCoy to give you boys. Here's twenty dollars for each man. I want to leave here day after tomorrow. Can you get the boys back by then?"

"I don't know about that." Bill twisted his hat brim around in his hands. "How about one more day?"

"I'll be leaving here at dawn day after tomorrow, Bill. Tell every man that wants his pay to be here ready to ride."

"I'll get them back here. Are you coming in?"

"Luke's going with you tonight. I'll stay here and look after the horses and the wagons and go in with you tomor-row night. I'll buy everybody a drink at the saloon, Bill. You men take care now."

King went to the wagon and dug out his last clean outfit and a towel. As he walked toward the creek, Juan approached him.

"Señor King, there is no cantina in this town. Eduardo and the *vaqueros* and I will stay with the wagons. Will you keep our money until we get back home?"

"I'll do that, Juan, sure. I'll see if I can find any tequila in this place. I'll just ride on in town for a little while tonight after all. I'll be coming back early. I'll bring you boys back something to drink."

"Gracias, *jefe.*"

King stripped and bathed in the creek, shivering in the cold water. He had lost weight on the drive. He had thinned out and his muscles felt as hard as a rock. Dressed in clean clothes and clean all over after days of eating dust behind cattle, King felt like a new man.

Luke and Cook stood beside the campfire. "Since them Mexicans are staying here to watch our stuff, I figured I'd go with you boys and see the sights," Cook said. He didn't appear to have bathed or changed; in fact, he looked as if he still had on the same shirt he wore when they left Blanco Sol. King and Luke exchanged long looks and turned to mount their horses.

It was dark when the group reached the saloon. The new hotel was directly across the wide street. Both buildings were full of light. They tied their horses in front of the saloon and went in.

The room was tremendous, painted a dark red with a high ceiling. Mirrors and paintings decorated the walls. Large round tables covered in green cloth were placed along three walls. A long polished bar ran along one side.

The Blanco Sol riders were clustered in one corner around a table. Neale and Henry Hastings both had girls sitting on their laps. As the group entered, the men whooped and yelled in greeting. They all appeared to be two or three drinks ahead. Cook joined the drovers and King and Luke chose a nearby table and ordered drinks.

One girl left Neale's lap and came over to put her hands on King's shoulder. "Do you want to dance, honey?" she asked, smiling into his eyes. King felt revulsion and disgust at the touch of the girl's hand. She was young and pretty. Her dark, heavy hair and smooth skin were beautiful, but her eyes seemed hard and knowing. King felt amazement at his reaction to her approach. He had known many girls like her in the past and always before had welcomed their advances.

He looked steadily back at the girl and said, "Maybe later, thanks. I've got some business to tend to over at the hotel." He rose from his chair. The girl turned away from him disdainfully and returned to her place in Neale's lap.

King nodded to Luke. "I think I'll go on back to camp. I promised the boys a drink. Here's enough money to treat the whole crew to a round on me." Leaving the saloon, he went to the store and purchased three bottles of liquor for the *vaqueros* and returned to the camp.

Spreading his blankets beside the fire, King sat down. Taking tobacco and paper from his pocket, he rolled a cigarette. His mind filled with the image of Sue Ellen. He had pushed thoughts of her away constantly on the trail, knowing he had to be alert and ready to handle anything to make it to Abilene. But he had finally won. He stayed in camp the next day and evening, hardly moving from his place by the fire except to make several inspection rides around the horses and wagons.

Not long after dark, the sound of horses roused him from his dreams. Luke and Neale rode into the light of the fire. They were holding Roy Jerdone on his horse between them. Fear hit King as he jumped to his feet. "What's wrong?" he asked.

Luke dismounted and pulled Roy from the saddle. "Roy here just got a little bump on his head. He's all right now." Roy stumbled over to sit by the fire. There was a big red bruise in the middle of his forehead.

"Did you have a fight? Tell me what happened. That's a nasty looking bruise you've got there." Luke and Neale began to hoot and laugh. Roy's face looked pained by more than the bruise. He was obviously terribly embarrassed.

"It ain't near as bad as it looks, boss. I'd be all right if those sorry hyenas would shut up their infernal laughing."

King smiled in spite of himself. "Will somebody please tell me what happened?"

Luke brought a cup and filled it with coffee. Squatting on his heels beside King, he grinned at Roy. "This here young rooster sashayed into the hotel and up and insulted a girl. She grabbed her a bottle and swatted him."

"Aw, Luke, that just ain't so and you know it. I only asked that girl if she would meet me later."

"That ain't the way it's done, kid. Ask King here."

King frowned at Luke. "Why tell him to ask me?" He struggled to keep from laughing out loud.

"King, I reckon it's yore fault that pore old Roy here got his head busted." Luke kept on grinning.

"My fault! How in the world do you figure it's my fault?"

"I think he figured to be the lady-killer of the outfit, since you give up the job. I reckon you owe it to him to give him some lessons before he runs up on a gal with a .44."

Neale and Luke fell to laughing again. King couldn't help joining in. Roy finally grinned sheepishly.

"He's right, boss. You could give me some advice."

King stopped laughing and stared thoughtfully at the boy. He was handsome. His hair and eyes were as pretty as a girl's. When he filled out, he would be a fine-looking man.

"I'll tell you this much. Girls are a puzzle, Roy. They love to turn a poor drover around their little fingers, but they like a man better if they can't. As I said, they're a downright puzzle. There's one thing I can say that might help you. Don't ever let on that they've got anything you might want. Just smile politely and look mysterious like you might have something they might want. Their natural curiosity will get them every time."

Bill Ewell and the rest of the riders made it back to camp about midnight. King let them sleep late into the morning. It was afternoon when they started for home.

The horse herd moved at its own pace without the cattle to hold them back. Each drover chose a different horse to ride every day. They figured it was the best way to make sure the mounts remembered they were working horses.

They met the first herd coming up the trail behind them

less than a week south of Abilene, then another every few days after that. Thousands of cattle passed by. Some were in herds as large as theirs had been and some were only a few hundred head. In the open areas, the trail widened to several miles as the cattle sought grass that hadn't been grazed over.

When the riders reached San Antonio, King went straight to the bank to deposit McCoy's draft and get enough cash to pay wages. As he returned to the wagons, he noticed that Windy Mason was standing with the Quivira bunch. King turned Ranger so he could dismount on the side away from the men and checked the loads in his Colt before he walked over to them.

"Gather 'round, boys. I've got your money here." The drovers clustered around King and he counted out their pay. He added a fifty-dollar bonus for each man.

Bill Ewell came up last to get his money. "We'll be saying goodbye here, King."

"I'm plumb sorry to hear that, Bill. I've got a place for you and these boys at Blanco Sol."

"I know, King, and I'm obliged, but Windy's here and we've all ridden together too long to break up the outfit now. Windy won't drink so bad without Matt around to egg him on. I reckon we'll all go ahead and stick together."

"I owe Mason wages, Bill. Here, you give this to him."

"You don't owe wages to a rider that don't finish a drive."

"Here, take it," King said, placing the money in Ewell's hand. "I fired the man. He didn't just leave. He worked for me and a man's got to eat."

"Well, I call that plumb decent of you, King. I know Windy will appreciate the money. You're a good man to ride for. White Sun will never want for riders."

King shook hands with each of the Quivira men, even Windy Mason. He was sad to see them leave. He had grown close to each of them in the long weeks on the trail.

Luke came to stand beside King as the group rode toward San Antonio. "We're going to miss those boys, King—particularly Bill Ewell. He's better with cattle than any rider I ever met."

King turned to place one hand on Luke's shoulder. "We made it, old son. We really made it. Let's get our business done and grab that preacher and go home."

Sending the outfit ahead toward the ranch with the wagons and horses, King and Luke rode into town to contact the preacher. He agreed to leave for the ranch the next morning. They spent the night in the hotel, grateful to sleep in a bed again.

The preacher's buggy waited in front of the hotel when Luke and King walked out the door. Judge Wilkerson sat on the seat beside the preacher. "Good morning, boys. I decided it was about time I got down to White Sun to see Lambert and Katherine, and there couldn't be a better chance for me to go. I'll make company for Reverend Dodson here on the way home after the weddings and he'll make company for me."

"Let's get this show on the road, then. I coulda been halfway home already if we left yesterday," said Luke.

They caught up with the wagons and remuda at Spanish Wells. It was a little late in the day, so they spent the night. King and Luke got up early the next morning and left Reverend Dodson and Judge Wilkerson with the wagons, riding on ahead.

They reached the ranch house not long after daybreak the following day. The courtyard was empty when they entered. Luke didn't say a word; he just waved his hand to King and headed across toward Sallie's door.

King entered the kitchen door quietly. Elena and Katherine were standing at the table preparing breakfast.

"King!" Katherine cried when she noticed him. The bowl she was holding clattered as it fell on the table. She ran to him. He caught her in his arms and held her tight.

"We didn't expect you for two more weeks at least." Katherine laughed and cried at the same time.

"We're here, Mother, and I'm starved." He looked over her head at Elena.

"Say, Elena, I'll kiss you too if you'll fix me a big plate of breakfast."

Elena giggled and blushed. "Sit down at the table here, Señor King. I'll have you some food pronto."

King wolfed down the plate full of potatoes and eggs and drank a second cup of coffee. He could feel the women watching him as he ate. He finally spoke again.

"How's Dad, Mother?"

"Oh, he's fine, honey. You'll be amazed. You'd never know he'd ever been sick."

"That's really great to hear. He'll be better yet when he hears how much I got for the cattle." King pushed back his chair and stood up. "I want to clean up some before I see Sue Ellen. I look worse than some scarecrows I've seen."

"Sue Ellen wouldn't even notice, son. But I'll get someone to bring you some hot water." Katherine's face glowed with happiness. King leaned over and kissed her again.

"Preacher Dodson and Judge Wilkerson will be here sometime tomorrow."

"Well, it's none too soon, I'd say," Katherine said, looking across the kitchen at Elena. "We'll be ready."

King left the room puzzled at his mother's tone. He rushed across the courtyard to his room. Stripping off his shirt, he sat down on the bed to pull off his ragged boots. They'd have to be thrown away. Two *vaqueros* brought a tub of steaming water and left it in the middle of the floor. They both grinned at King and waved a hand but didn't speak.

King soaked in the bath, relishing the clean feeling of the hot, soapy water. When satisfied he'd removed all the trail dust, he got out of the tub and dressed, toweling his long hair partly dry. Clean-shaven and dressed in a complete outfit of new clothes down to his boots, he picked up his hat and opened the door.

Sue Ellen stood in front of his door with her hand raised as though ready to knock. King grinned down at her and said, "Did you miss me, sweetheart?"

She dropped her head against his chest. "I was almost afraid you were never coming out of your room."

Drawing her into his arms, he kissed her and held her close. After a moment, she raised her head and looked up at him with accusing eyes. "You didn't care enough about me to come to me first. I heard something and when I looked outside, Luke was holding Sallie and they were both crying."

King laughed and said, "You're jealous, that's what's the matter with you, Sue Ellen Shepherd."

"He at least shows he loves her. She's been as contented as a cat the whole time you and Luke have been gone." She sounded almost angry.

"I'm downright ashamed of you, honey. Why should Sallie be so sure of Luke and you doubt me?"

"Sallie's carrying Luke's child." Her cheeks flamed as she hid her face against him.

"What!" King was astounded and delighted. He laughed down at Sue Ellen. She was staring at him as if spellbound.

"That's the reason why you're so jealous, isn't it?" he asked softly, watching her eyes.

"Stop that, you—you wild drover. I'm surprised at you."

She pulled out of his arms and moved a few steps away, her eyes dancing. "Come on with me, King. Your father sent me to get you. He wants to hear all about the drive."